SOMETHING TO THINK ABOUT

Whiskey Mountain Book 2

Samantha Baca

Whiskey Mountain

Whiskey Mountain Series

Something To Talk About
Something To Think About
Something To Believe In
Something To Live For

Content Warning

Please note that this book may contain subject matter that may be bothersome for some readers. Please contact the author directly if you have any questions or need guidance before reading this book.

Suicide—mention of and with a secondary character. Not described in detail.

Mental health—touches on depression, anxiety, and suicide mentioned above.

Contents

<u>One</u>

Ramona

"I'll take the number three, hold the Pico de Gallo, and add a side of queso."

I rolled my eyes and shifted my weight while I waited for the guy in front of me to finish ordering. It wasn't just his tall 6'2 frame that irritated me; it was that there was zero fat on his lean, muscular body and that he had an ass so tight that you could crack a nut on it.

"Can I get a name for your order?" the girl behind the counter asked, her voice obnoxiously sweet and flirty.

"Preston."

My eye twitched as his deep voice rumbled across the air, sending a jolt to my stomach. It was the same stupid smooth tone that had all the women in Whiskey Mountain tossing their panties at him, except for me. Kind of like he thought he was God's gift to women or something. Spoiler alert—he wasn't.

He finally stepped to the side, took the number card the other girl handed him while batting her eyes, and got the hell out of my way.

"Hi, what can I get you?"

I narrowed my eyes at her, more than slightly miffed that her tone wasn't as cheerful with me as it was with him. *Well, excuse me for not being the symbol of a fucking sex God.*

"I'd like a number 5, extra sour cream, extra guacamole, and a side of queso."

I felt him watching me, his judgmental gaze speaking more than words could ever say.

"To drink?"

"Diet Coke." I hated Diet Coke and wanted a Root Beer float but having Mr. Perfect Body without an ounce of fat on his ridiculous body made me self-conscious, knowing he was criticizing what I had ordered.

The girl punched the information into the computer and then handed me my receipt with a fake smile that she probably used for everyone she didn't want to get laid by. Little did she know—I was a fucking fantastic lay. Her loss, not that I would do her, anyway.

I moved on and waited off to the side, as far away from him as possible, while they prepared my food. Maggie and Dylan were already here and waiting for me at a table tucked in the back of La Salsa. In the meantime, I was trying to shake off the sour mood I was in before I joined them. No need to ruin everyone else's day, too.

A few orders were up before mine, and then, finally, my number was called. I went to reach for the tray at the same time *Preston* did, pulling my hand away as quickly as possible when I realized we were about to touch.

"Excuse me, that's my order," I blurted out, placing a hand on my hip when he refused to let go of the tray.

"I don't think so. Yours has a deep-fried chimichanga and plenty of artery-clogging sides. This one is mine. Number 69—see?" He held the card up next to the receipt on the tray and waved it at me.

My eyes narrowed again, making me wish I had some sort of superpower to shoot laser beams out of them and light him on fire.

Being this close to him made me feel like I couldn't breathe. It wasn't just the cedary scent of his cologne that permeated the air around me; it was something deeper than that. Something that I didn't have the time to process—nor did I want to.

Before I could say anything or defend my food choices, he tossed me a wink before grabbing the tray and brushing past me, sending another spark through me.

What the fuck was that about?

I felt like an idiot for not hearing the number right the first time. Maybe I was just so hungry that I had imagined they'd called my number instead of his. It made sense that his would be ready before mine since he was in line in front of me, and I saw him still standing there before I almost stole his food.

I focused on pulling slow, calming breaths in through my nose and exhaling them through pursed lips while waiting for my food. My stomach growled again, reminding me I had skipped breakfast and was officially in the *danger zone*.

Finally, my order was up, so I grabbed the tray—double-checked that the number on the receipt matched the card I was holding—and headed to join Maggie and Dylan at the table.

I must have still been scowling by the time I sat down because they both stopped talking and stared at me.

"What?" I asked grumpily before pulling my chair closer to the table and popping a tortilla chip into my mouth. I couldn't tell if I was still just grumpy or if being hangry had taken over completely.

"Nothing," Maggie said, lifting her hands in front of her.

"Someone is hangry today," Dylan murmured to her from the side of his mouth, trying to keep me from hearing it.

"Shut up." I squirted some hot sauce onto my chimichanga and lifted it to take a bite when a perfectly buzzed cut head caught my attention from a few tables over. I lowered the food back to my plate and snarled.

"Uh oh." Dylan scooted away from the table as if he was afraid that I might flip it.

Maggie's eyes followed mine, the confusion not lasting long.

"Oh, come on, Ramona," she laughed. "Are you seriously that upset over Preston? He's just having lunch."

"It's not that he's here having lunch," I bit out. "It's that he's *everywhere*. It doesn't matter where I go or what I do—he's there."

"You know that's how living in a small-town works, right?" Maggie's smile was meant to disarm me, but it only fueled the fire raging inside me.

"Yeah, but he's not from *this one*. He's from Fallen Oaks and needs to go back to where he came from."

"Fallen Oaks is only a half hour from here—forty-five minutes, tops," Dylan said before ducking as I tossed a piece of napkin at his head.

"Whatever," I growled. "It doesn't matter where he came from. It matters that he doesn't need to be everywhere that I am. He's always slowing the lines down and causing delays because he's *so good-looking*." I rolled my eyes again, feeling completely childish for using such a mocking tone.

"Are you interested in him?" Maggie asked, her eyes dancing with delight.

"No."

"Are you sure? Because it seems like you might."

"NO," I repeated louder, drawing the attention of a few people close by, but thankfully not Preston. "YOU can love love, but that doesn't mean the rest of us have to."

"You're abnormally grumpy about love," Dylan commented, his eyebrows pulled together.

"Today would have been her and Daniel's anniversary." Maggie attempted to whisper behind her hand, but I could still hear her.

"Oh, shit."

"It's not a big deal," I lied. "We were together for three years. *I* broke up with *him*."

"Have you talked to him?" Maggie asked softly.

"Not since he called a few weeks ago to ask if I had one of his stupid PlayStation games."

"Why would you have it?" Maggie lifted her burrito to take a bite while she waited for my answer.

"Because he's Daniel and loses shit all the time. The same Daniel who refuses to take responsibility for anything and blames everyone else for the things that go wrong in his life."

"Yeah, but *you* moved out of the house. Why would he think that you would take his stuff? He's the one who kept the house and 90% of everything in it."

"Don't remind me," I said bitterly, sliding down lower in my chair. I poked at the chimichanga, suddenly not having the same appetite as I did when I first ordered the massive plate full of food.

"You're better off without him," Dylan said, locking eyes with me.

"I know," I sighed heavily. "Just when I was getting used to being single, this stupid date snuck up on me, and the gift I bought for him months before we broke up showed up at the store this morning. I had forgotten about it until I opened it up."

"What was it?" Maggie asked, looking down to check her phone.

"A collection of these exotic jerkies and assorted cheese and crackers. It was meant to go with the all-day gaming weekend I had planned for him—which should have been a sign that our relationship was doomed from the start if I focused only on *him* and what made him happy when I bought his gift."

"I'm sorry," Maggie apologized, her eyes softening.

"It's fine. I'm fine. Everything is fine."

I scooped a spoonful of guacamole out of the bowl and started smothering the chimichanga with it when I caught someone next to me out of the corner of my eye.

Preston tossed his trash in the trashcan before setting the basket and tray on top. He looked my way, gave me a devilish smile as if he knew how much it would get under my skin, then walked out the door.

My blood pressure rose a notch as I stabbed a giant piece of guac-covered chimichanga and shoved it into my mouth.

<u>Two</u>

Preston

"Why did you get a dog if you didn't have time to take care of it?" I asked my mom, patting the giant labradoodle's head as it panted heavily.

"Your dad was lonely, and I've been busy with work, so I thought it was a good idea." She shrugged and walked around the kitchen, looking for the spices she needed for the meatloaf.

"Why didn't you get a small lap dog? This thing is way too big for Dad and has too much energy. You need to take him for walks and get daily exercise."

"I've tried, but he doesn't want to get off the couch."

"The dog?"

"No, your dad."

I shook my head and laughed.

"Seriously, Mom. What were you thinking?"

"I don't know," she sighed, stopping what she was doing as she turned around and looked at me. "I thought if I got a big dog that was full of energy, it would keep your dad happy, and he wouldn't be so depressed anymore."

"He lost a job he's had for over thirty years, Mom. He's bound to be depressed for a while. Plus, I can't imagine how he feels knowing you're the only one bringing money into the house right now. He's a prideful man whose ego is taking one hell of a beating."

"I know. In hindsight, getting Rosco might not have been the best idea. But I was desperate, Preston. I wanted my husband back. I wanted to see the wrinkles around his lips as he smiled. I wanted to hear him laugh again. I've missed all of it so much, and I was afraid I would lose him."

"I get it. I do. Have you told Kent about this?"

"No, and you better not before I can talk to him." She wagged her finger at me as she went back to working on the meatloaf.

"Fine, I won't tell him. But you better get around to it before he comes to town to visit and finds this behemoth of a creature eating your couch."

"I talked with him briefly the other day, and he mentioned he was busy helping with some B&B project. I don't think we'll see him for a couple of weeks."

"I don't know. I wouldn't count on it. It's not like Fallen Oaks is that long of a drive. And you know Kent, he likes to surprise people."

My mom turned around; her face twisted in an attempted smile.

"That's why I need your help."

"With what?" I asked, knowing it must be big because my mother *never* asked for help.

"Just a *little* favor." She held her fingers apart to show me how small it was.

"I have a feeling it's not little at all," I sighed, adjusting on the barstool I was sitting on as I braced myself for whatever she was about to ask for.

"I need you to take Rosco for a while."

"You're kidding me, right?"

"I wish I were, but now that I see you with him, it just seems like he's a better fit for you than he is for us."

"How long have you had him?"

"Two days."

"And you're not even going to give it a try first?"

"Who was I kidding, Preston?" She sighed and leaned against the counter. "You and I both know that your dad and I aren't cut out for a pet. Deep down, I guess I hoped you would come in here and tell me I was right and that I did the right thing for your dad by getting him a dog. But I could tell the moment you saw it that you didn't feel that way, and I guess it just made me realize how big of a mistake I made."

"Yeah, Mom. It's a dog—not a toy. It has actual needs, and you shouldn't have bought it without thinking about all of that first."

"I know, I know. I feel terrible. But I can't take him back to the place I got him, and I don't want to give him to just anyone. Even if you don't believe me, I love Rosco and want him to have a good home. Even if I can't give it to him."

"Is this why you invited me over?" I closed my eyes and pinched the bridge of my nose between my fingers.

This was all too much. I just came to check on my parents, maybe have a glass of my mom's famous sweet tea, and possibly score some meatloaf before I left now that I knew she was making my favorite meal.

I *didn't* expect to come by and leave as the proud new owner of some giant dog.

"Maybe…" Her voice teetered. "I know that it's a lot to ask, but I know you can handle it. You have that great big backyard he can run in. Plus, you work from home, so you'll be there to keep an eye on him. And not to make you feel bad, but it gives me a little satisfaction to know that you're not sitting there alone all the time, bored and lonely."

"I enjoy being alone," I said defiantly. "There's nothing wrong with being single."

"No, but you're almost—"

"Twenty-five? That's not old, Mom."

"I didn't say it was," she objected. "I just meant that I would like to see you find someone and settle down. Fall in love. Have a family."

"And a dog?"

My lips curled into a smile as the dog thumped its tail against the wooden floor.

I tried to look away and pretend that I wasn't affected by this damn dog, but once its beady brown eyes locked on mine, I couldn't.

Three

Ramona

"Yes, I've tried restarting the computer." I gritted my teeth, frustrated that this was the fourth IT support person I had spoken to who had no flipping idea what was happening with my computer. "It works for a little bit and then crashes."

I pressed the palm of my hand against my forehead and closed my eyes. If I couldn't get my computer to work right, then I couldn't keep my business open since I wouldn't be able to process sales. But more importantly—I couldn't stalk Maggie's blog page for more *Just The Tip* posts. I was single, but that didn't mean that I wasn't keeping up on all the sexual advice she gave there or that I didn't submit a question or two myself every now and then.

I waited impatiently while the person on the other end of the phone did something on their side—for all I knew, they were Googling how to fix a computer. Everyone I talked to seemed to have no clue how to solve the problem and kept sending me to someone else because they didn't want to bother figuring it out.

The clock on the wall above my head ticked loudly, reminding me I needed to open Cool Cats soon. The nice thing about owning a pet store was that it was doubling as my house since I couldn't afford to get my own place right now.

When I first left Daniel, I stayed with Maggie for a few weeks while I worked on converting the storage room into a bedroom. It was a decent-sized room once I got all the big boxes out of it, and thankfully everything fit so I didn't have to rent a storage unit. Dylan and Maggie had come by and helped me convert the two single bathrooms into one large bathroom with a tub/shower combo and a decent-sized vanity with plenty of storage.

The kitchen was already set up from when my great-grandparents owned the building and ran a small restaurant with a speakeasy bar in the back. I had been using the space as a break room but decided to update the appliances and flooring once it became my new kitchen. It was now fully functional, and I could technically say that I worked from home.

After fifteen minutes of waiting for IT support to confirm they had no idea what was happening with my computer, I gave up and ended the phone call. Thankfully, I was able to go online from my phone and set up the password for today. Granted, it wasn't technically *needed,* and the only reason I even required a password to enter was to keep the speakeasy vibe alive. I loved hearing the stories passed down from generation to generation about our family's history and wanted to keep the fun part of it going.

I loved that aside from the locals, no one knew that Cool Cats existed just from looking at the building. I had been open long enough that everyone in Whiskey Mountain and Fallen Oaks knew that they would have to go online, solve a riddle, and then they would be given the password for the day. Once they had it, they could either place an order online or come into the store.

I wrote *Drunken Dogs on Broken Logs* on a piece of paper that I kept by the speaker, so I didn't have to constantly pull it up on my phone when people came by. Not that I had a ton of customers, but every now and then, I was surprised by a busy day.

It was just after nine, and the meteorologist on the TV mounted in the corner of the room was talking about a massive storm headed for Whiskey Mountain. It wasn't unusual to get bad weather here, but it was definitely sooner than we usually got it—especially with a storm of this magnitude. I turned up the volume and listened as he went on about the possibility of getting 10-15 inches of snow this weekend—if not more.

I couldn't remember the last time I'd seen 10-15 inches of anything—snow or cock. Hell, I was lucky even to get a full *six* with Daniel, and that was when I got his full attention and he wasn't focused on getting back to his damn video game.

I debated whether I needed to head out and get supplies now or if I could wait a few days. It wasn't like I would need much since it was just me, but since Cool Cats was in the middle of nowhere, that didn't leave me many options if I ran out of something.

While Cool Cats was technically in Fallen Oaks, it didn't matter. All of Montana was going to get walloped, and I was going to be shit out of luck if I didn't get to the store now. If I waited too long, I would either risk everyone beating me there and be faced with empty shelves, or I would get stuck in the storm and wouldn't be allowed back on the highway to get to Cool Cats until they got a plow out there to clear the roads. Since it was in a deserted spot located between two small towns, it wasn't ever a priority when they worked on clearing the streets because people didn't tend to pass through during bad weather unless they absolutely had to.

I pulled out my phone, logged into the site, and posted a note that we would open later today. I grabbed my keys and wallet, then locked up and headed to Super Seven, the only supermarket in Whiskey Mountain.

By the time I got there, the parking lot was full, and almost all the shopping carts were taken. I pulled my shoulders back and tried to remind myself that everyone was there because they all needed supplies as well. I smiled politely at an old man who was shuffling his way to the cart return after unloading his bags into his car.

I looked around, trying not to make him feel rushed as I kept my distance. He walked past and gave me a quick wave before climbing into the car parked at the curb with his wife inside. I inhaled deeply, ready to get this over with.

I headed to the cart corral and reached for the one he'd just left, my hand brushing against someone else's as they grabbed it too.

I didn't have to look up to see who it was because the electrical shock that zapped my skin from the touch of his hand on mine had already told me that it was Preston.

"Sorry," I muttered before I could stop myself. It was more out of habit than anything. I didn't *really* want to apologize to him since I had been there first, and like always, he was in my way again.

"No, I'm sorry. I didn't see you there. Go ahead. You can have it."

I eyed him suspiciously, wondering why he was being nice.

"Really. Take it."

There was an impatience in his tone that dug its way under my skin as he shoved a hand through his short black hair.

"Thanks, since I *was* waiting for it first."

His gray eyes scanned my face as if trying to figure something out.

Irritated from the feeling he elicited every time he was this close, I grabbed the cart, yanked it out of the corral, and shoved it in front of me.

He grinned that stupid grin that seemed to work for everyone but me.

I didn't bother to look back to see if he was still standing there, staring at me. I had stuff to get done, and it didn't involve him.

The aisles were busy, but thankfully, people were quick to grab what they needed and move on. No one was shopping for fun or dilly-dallying around and taking their time. They knew this storm was coming, and no one trusted the weather in Montana to come when they predicted it, so they wanted to be as prepared as possible since it could be on us at any moment.

I grabbed a family-sized pack of toilet paper and shoved it on the bottom rack of the shopping cart, then grabbed another—just in case. My cart was packed with canned goods, non-perishable items, and basic necessities. Okay, so maybe coffee, Cool Ranch Doritos, Milk Duds, and Hot Tamales weren't necessities for anyone else, but they were for me. Just because we were going to have a record-breaking storm hit didn't mean that I couldn't indulge in some of my favorite treats.

I was perusing the wine aisle, looking for the cheap brand that I liked. It wasn't that I was opposed to spending money on a good bottle, but if the power went out—like it was known to do with bad storms—I wanted to be able to open a bottle with a screw-on top instead of messing with trying to use a bottle opener in the dark.

The alcohol section was quieter than the rest of the store, so I didn't pay attention that someone was standing at the end of the aisle while I was squatting to retrieve a bottle of Moscato on the bottom shelf that had been shoved to the back. I reached a little further, trying not to fall, when I heard a chuckle.

I looked up to see Preston watching me, amusement etched on his face. I bit my tongue to keep from saying anything while he looked at the expensive bottles of whiskey. I didn't need his judgment right now with my cheap bottles of wine, just like I didn't need it the other day with my order at La Salsa.

The bottle was just within reach as I scooted closer, leaning to the side and brushing against Preston's leg. I hadn't noticed that he had moved toward me until I was practically pressed into his leg, trying to grab the damn wine. I was about to say something to him about giving me space when I heard a familiar voice from the other end of the aisle.

"Always a sucker for those cheap bottles," Daniel said, tsking as he walked over to where I was still crouched on the ground with my hand wrapped around it.

I thought about pulling it out and whipping it at his head, but I didn't want to waste the only bottle of Moscato they had.

My heart raced, having to face Daniel for the first time since we broke up. He'd called and texted a handful of times over the past six months, but I ignored almost every single one.

"Why don't you just grab one of the better bottles? I'll get it for you, my treat. I know how *hard* things must be with you trying to do this on your own right now." A smug grin was plastered on Daniel's face as he leaned against a pole at the end of the aisle and watched me.

I looked up at Preston, embarrassed that he was standing there, hearing all of this. But since he was already a part of it—whether he wanted to be or not—I decided to use what I had at my disposal right now, even if I would later regret it.

I pushed up to a standing position and leaned in so only he could hear me.

"Pretend to be my boyfriend, or I'll break this bottle and cut your internal organs out with its jagged edge," I threatened, looking up to meet his eyes.

He licked his lips and let the bottom catch between his teeth. I could tell he was trying to keep from laughing, which further irritated me.

"You know I would have gotten that for you, baby," he said sweetly, gently wrapping his hand around mine as he relieved me from my weapon. He put it in his cart and then wrapped one arm around my waist, making sure our bodies were angled so Daniel could see it.

"Sorry," Daniel said, clearing his throat. "I didn't know you were here with someone."

His apology lacked genuine emotion, and I was pretty sure it wasn't directed at me.

I felt Preston's fingers dig deeper into my hip before his hand slid possessively across my stomach as he pulled me closer. My body was on fire from his touch, my senses on overload.

What in the world was this? Why did his touch elicit such powerful responses from my body?

"We better get going, Firecracker. That storm is moving in quickly, and we don't want to get stuck in it."

My brain was mush at the moment, trying to process what he was saying as his hand slipped from my waist and his fingers brushed across my ass.

"Firecracker?" Daniel questioned with a smirk. He hated pet names, so I knew he was going to take this opportunity to tell Preston how stupid they were. "Let me guess; you call her that because of her fiery temper?"

My face flushed with embarrassment. It wasn't like it was a lie—Preston would know that given how I'd treated him the handful of times we'd interacted with each other.

"Na, I call her that because I love the way she lights up when she comes. The way her body is on fire, ready for me to send her over the edge. Reminds me of the Fourth of July, and I just can't get enough of it."

He winked at Daniel, whose jaw was hanging as he processed what Preston said.

"If you want to grab the lube, chocolate syrup, and whipped cream, I'll meet you at the register," Preston added, giving me a sharp slap on the ass before releasing his grip on me. "Gotta make the best out of being cooped up in the house during the storm," he added, looking Daniel directly in the eye.

"Yeah, sure." I had no idea what to say. My brain was in a fog, and my ass was still burning from his touch. There was also this new ache building between my thighs that made me acutely aware of how close Preston was as I pushed the cart down the aisle and headed for the frozen food section.

Once we were out of sight of Daniel, I pushed my cart to the side and spun around to face him. He was sporting a shit-eating grin on his face, and his shoulders pulled back like he was proud of himself.

"What in the hell was that?!" I hissed, my eyes nearly bulging out of my head.

"*That* was me saving *your* ass and avoiding a shanking on aisle 3."

"You didn't have to slap my ass."

"Did you want him to buy it or not?"

"Yes, but—"

He leaned in and wrapped one hand behind my head while the other cupped the side of my face. His mouth crashed down on mine in the most gentle yet hungry kiss I'd ever experienced. His lips moved eagerly as his tongue slid across my lips.

Reluctantly, they parted, allowing his tongue to dance with mine. I reached up and wrapped my arms around his neck, pulling him closer while trying to refrain from wrapping my legs around his waist and riding him on aisle 5.

My pussy ached with need, my panties already soaked as I panted against his mouth when he broke the kiss too soon.

I opened my eyes, trying to force myself to focus, but all I could concentrate on right now was kissing him again.

"You're welcome," he said cockily.

"What?" I panted, my breaths ragged and shallow. I tilted my head to the side and studied him.

"I can't promise seven orgasms, but I think we know for a fact that you'll have at least five tonight." His voice was louder than necessary. "Though I'm always up for a challenge."

I squinted my eyes, having no clue what was going on. Did he kiss me so hard that he sucked all the brain cells out of my body? Was that a thing?

"He's on the aisle over. I think he's trying to get you alone to talk to you."

Oh. Fuck.

"Sorry," I whispered, though I had no idea what I was apologizing for.

"If you want to keep this up, we need to leave together and look like a happy couple, which means you're going to have to refrain from threatening to kill me until *after* we leave."

"Fine," I sighed. "I'm pretty much done. What about you?"

"I just have a few things left to get. Want to meet at the registers in ten minutes?"

I nodded and waited for him to go ahead of me so I could take a deep breath and try to calm my nerves. Never in a million years would I have ever imagined that I would be kissing Preston in the aisle of a grocery store while trying to avoid my ex, but here we were.

<u>Four</u>

Preston

I barely made it to the house I was renting before the snow started falling. I still needed to get food and supplies for Rosco, but they didn't have much at the supermarket. Not only that, but I got super distracted by Ramona and her constant threat of bodily harm if I didn't pretend to be her boyfriend.

I didn't know her well—mainly because she always looked like she was ready to kill me whenever we were around each other, so it left little opportunity for friendly conversation. But I didn't have to know her well to know that her attitude was bigger than her 5'2 self. Between the way her eyes constantly narrowed when she looked at me and the frown that always graced her face, I couldn't imagine that we would ever be the *best of friends* before I left Whiskey Mountain.

Rosco ran around the kitchen, pacing beside me as if he expected I had something for him, which I didn't. He was still a puppy; my mom had gotten him at eight weeks, so it had only been a few days since he'd been separated from his mom and siblings. I could tell that we would have a lot of work ahead of us with learning obedience, given that he had chewed up a pair of my shoes while I was at the store.

"You sure have a lot of energy, don't you, boy?" I scratched the top of his head as he stretched his legs and then rolled over so I could rub his stomach. "That storm is moving in quickly, so I need to get to the store before they close. Otherwise, you won't have food for a few days."

He whimpered and pawed at my hand as I pulled away to stand up.

I had looked up pet stores in town and found that the only one close by was one called Cool Cats, and it was at least an hour from where I was staying, right on the border of Whiskey Mountain and the neighboring small town, Fallen Oaks. The storm was going to get worse before it got better, and I didn't want to start Rosco on people food, so I needed to get going before I got stuck in it.

I grabbed my keys and thought about whether I should lock him up somewhere to keep him from destroying anything while I was gone, but it wasn't like I'd had time to puppy-proof the house. It didn't say online whether animals were allowed inside Cool Cats, only that you had to have a password to get in. Deciding that it was better to keep Rosco with me so I could keep an eye on him, I attached the leash to the collar my mom had got him and led him out to my truck.

He climbed in easily, needing only a tiny bit of help. Then he plopped down on the leather seat and closed his eyes while the seat warmer did its magic. I laughed and shook my head, wondering how I got myself into this position.

I had a big heart and was a sucker for cute animals—that's how I got here.

An hour later, I slowed down as I pulled up in front of an unmarked building. I leaned forward, squinting to look for a sign, but I couldn't see anything through the thick snow falling around me. I circled the building, looking for any sign that I was in the right place, but aside from one lonely vehicle in the parking lot, there wasn't much to go off of.

I knew that it was a huge risk to head out in the storm. But unfortunately, it was either brave it and trust that my truck could handle the weather to get me to the store and back or share the food I had picked up for myself with Rosco and start a bad habit that I wouldn't be able to break.

I got out of the truck and walked around to get him. The temperature had already dropped significantly, so there was no way I was going to leave him in the truck while I went inside to grab stuff. Hopefully it would be a quick and easy trip, then we would be home and warmed by the fire.

I walked to the call box and pressed the button, shoving my hands in my pockets to keep warm. I wasn't sure if Cool Cats was even open since everything else seemed to shut down early because of the weather. I was about to leave and head back to the truck when I heard a voice come over the speaker.

"Hello?"

"Hi. Sorry to bother you. I was looking for Cool Cats. It's a pet—"

"What's the password?"

I pulled the piece of torn-off paper out of my pocket and unfolded it.

"Drunken dogs on broken logs," I answered, taken aback by the person's inhospitable vibe. While I knew a password was required to enter, I was still shocked that this was considered a business, given how unfriendly they were acting.

There was a loud beeping noise, and then I heard the lock click. I pulled the door open and headed down the stairs, wondering if this was a legit pet shop or if it was some shady business where they murdered unsuspecting victims coming in for dog treats. Guess I was about to find out.

I rounded the corner with Rosco leading the way, trying to gain control over him on the leash.

"Slow down," I said, pulling it back. "You're going to take me down if you don't stop."

"Wouldn't be such a bad thing," a feisty voice answered, a pile of raven black hair piled loosely on her head.

Something about the snark in Ramona's tone sent a chill throughout my body. I wasn't sure whether it was fear or excitement, but it was there, nonetheless.

"So, we're back to that again?" I teased, attempting to keep Rosco from jumping on her as she squatted in front of a shelf that she was stocking with fish food.

"Back to what?" She frowned, her hazel eyes catching in the light above us.

"You wanting to kill me."

"Maybe." She stood up and eyed me suspiciously before looking down at Rosco. "What are you doing here?"

"I came for supplies."

"Whose dog is this?"

"Mine."

"Are you sure you didn't steal it from someone?" she asked, folding her arms over her chest. The red and black flannel shirt she was wearing unbuttoned over a tight-fitting tank top did nothing to hide the curves I'd felt earlier when I wrapped my arm around her waist. I hadn't noticed it earlier, given it was hidden under a big, bulky winter jacket.

"Why would I steal someone's dog?"

"So you'd have an excuse to come see me."

"You're kidding me, right?" I laughed, wondering what in the world was going on inside of that head of hers.

"Not one bit."

"Look," I sighed, shoving a hand through my hair. "I didn't even know you worked here. I just googled pet shops in Whiskey Mountain, and this was the only one that came up."

"I don't just *work* here. I own the place. And it's convenient that you show up with a dog and *need supplies* a few hours after you were just groping me in the supermarket."

She took a step toward me, her features flawless as she narrowed those gorgeous hazel eyes at me. Again.

"You needed me to," I countered.

"You wanted to."

Now it was my turn to feel flustered because she wasn't lying. I had wanted to and might have taken advantage of the situation to get the point across to her asshole ex.

I stepped toward her, so close that our bodies were almost touching and I could feel the heat coming off hers.

"I did, and I would do it again in a heartbeat if you'd let me," I admitted, my voice low and gruff.

She licked her lips, making me want to capture one between my teeth.

Her mouth opened like she was going to say something, but Rosco chose that time to yank forward on the leash, slamming my body into hers. I wrapped an arm around her waist and spun her to the side so her back was up against the shelf, my leg pinned in between hers to keep us from falling.

"He has a lot of energy," I apologized.

"He needs to be trained."

"I'm planning on it."

We stood there staring at each other, neither of us moving apart as the heat of our bodies spread between us.

"What did you need?" she finally asked, but my brain was focused on how her lips looked as they moved and not the words that came out of them.

She arched an eyebrow in irritation when I didn't answer her.

"What?"

"From the store. What did you need from the store?" she clarified, pushing a hand against my chest to separate us.

I stepped back, giving her some space as I tried not to trip over Rosco's leash.

"I can help you grab what you need so you can get going," Ramona said, pushing away from the shelf and walking in front of me. "That storm is getting worse, and if you don't get back soon, you're going to get stranded. Since there's nothing within miles of here, we don't want that to happen, now do we?"

"Right." I shook my head to clear it. "My mom got him for my dad and didn't think about how much work a puppy this size would be. She's had him for two days and gave me what she was given by the lady she bought him from, which wasn't much. So, I need everything—food, a bed, treats, toys, and anything else you can think of that I might be forgetting."

"Okay, let's get started." Ramona clapped her hands and took off down the aisles as Rosco and I followed behind her. I couldn't tell if she was excited to shop for dog stuff or more excited to get it over with so she could get rid of us.

Five

Ramona

"Are you sure you don't want another bag of treats?" I asked, trying not to look into the golden eyes of the boy who was begging me for another one as I rang his dad up.

"No, I think we're fine. I want him to earn them and not just get them because he's cute."

"But he is cute," I objected, refraining from digging in the jar for another one.

He raised an eyebrow and tilted his head.

"Okay, fine." I sighed heavily and entered the last few things into the system. "Alright, your total is…"

I waited impatiently for it to pop up on the screen but was instead greeted by the spinning wheel of death.

"Everything okay?" he asked, leaning to the side to look at the screen. "Did I buy so much that I broke your register?"

"No, it just does this," I muttered, tapping the refresh button with my nail repeatedly, hoping it would force it to work.

"Do you want me to pay with cash instead?"

"No, because I don't have the exact total for you, and most likely, I won't have the right change. Besides, who is walking around with that much cash? I don't know the exact number, but I can tell you that you're around $250, at minimum."

I couldn't remember the last time someone came in and spent that much at Cool Cats, aside from my best friend, Maggie, who bought the most expensive terrarium so her panty-eating turtle couldn't escape anymore. But Preston had frowned when I showed him a decent-sized dog bed for Rosco and insisted on getting the bigger one with a thick layer of memory foam and was lined with sherpa.

"I'm not that worried about the change. I don't want to stress you out with your system not working."

"It never works these days," I grumbled, jabbing my finger harder on the screen. "I've been trying to get it fixed, but no one seems to know what's wrong with it."

"Mind if I come around and take a look?" he offered.

"You know about computers?" I tried to keep the sarcasm out of my voice, but it felt like regardless of what I said to him, it always came out super bitchy. I guess he just had that effect on me.

"I know a thing or two." His grin was smug, but I didn't have time to read too much into it if I wanted to get him out the door and on his way before he was stuck here.

"Be my guest."

I stepped back and made room for him to come around the counter. His brows pinched together as he studied the screen while moving the mouse that wouldn't work.

He pressed a few buttons and I thought for a minute that maybe he had fixed it when the screen refreshed and went to the payment window, but a few seconds later, everything went black, and it did the same thing it had been doing.

"Ugh," I groaned, tossing my head back. "I'm so tired of that stupid black screen of death."

"How long has it been doing this?" he asked, looking at me

over his shoulder.

"I don't know. A week? Maybe two."

"Have you run any updates recently?"

I scrunched my face as I tried to remember the last time it updated.

"I think it did one a few weeks ago."

"Okay, that might be what's causing this. I can try to do a system restore if you know approximately when that was."

"It's okay, I don't want to keep you here longer than needed. You'll never get home if you don't leave soon. Why don't you take what you have, and we can figure out the payment details later?"

"I'm not leaving here without paying for my stuff."

"Well, that's going to be hard because I don't know how much you owe me. Plus, it's not like you're going to skip town and I'll never see you again. I mean, you're already everywhere I go as it is."

My face reddened as I realized what I'd just said out loud. The corners of his lips twitched as he tried to hide a smile.

"Just take this, and we'll deal with the payment part later."

I was desperate for him to leave, but for once, it didn't feel like it was because he was annoying me. Instead, I was feeling a little more friendly with him and that was an unsettling feeling that I needed to get rid of as much as I needed to get rid of him.

"Fine," he sighed as he pulled his wallet out and tossed three-hundred-dollar bills on the counter.

"Preston," I objected, but he lifted a finger and placed it over my lips to stop me.

"Thank you for staying open so I could grab what I needed," he said, letting his finger trail across my skin as it slid down my lip and brushed against my cheek. "Take that for what I owe you for the supplies."

"This is too much."

"Well then, consider the extra to be a tip."

"A tip? I'm not a waitress," I sniped.

"That's probably a good thing." His stupid cocky grin spread across his cheeks again.

"What's that supposed to mean?" I planted a hand firmly on my hip and glared at him.

"That I'm glad you don't have access to my food or drink because I'm pretty sure you would have tried to poison me by now."

The corners of my lips twitched as I refused to let him see me smile.

"But seriously, thank you for staying open and letting me get the things we needed. Sorry to keep you so late."

"No problem."

I helped him grab the bags he couldn't carry and followed him up the stairs. He set his down and opened the door, only to have it flung against the wall as a gust of wind and snow blew in our faces, nearly taking our breath away.

I lifted my arm to shield myself from it and looked around for his truck, but the entire parking lot was covered in snow, and we couldn't see more than a few feet in front of us.

"Um, where did you park?" I asked nervously.

"Right there, up front." He pointed to a spot nearby, but neither of us could see it. "Fuck."

Fuck was right. There was no way he was going anywhere in this weather which meant he was now stuck here with me.

32

<u>Six</u>

Preston

I knew that I didn't have much time before the storm rolled in, but I thought for sure that I had enough to get the stuff I needed for Rosco and get home before this happened. We stood there for a few seconds, staring in disbelief at the whiteout in front of us before I fumbled around, reaching for the door and pulling it closed.

When I turned around, Ramona was standing behind me, the bags on the floor by her side while she nervously chewed her nails.

"I'm sorry. I thought I would make it out before it got that bad."

"It's okay," she said, but I could tell her mind was elsewhere. Her tone was clipped but not drooling with anger like it usually was.

"Do you know when they'll be out to plow the road?" I asked, already knowing the answer. No one was going out in this anytime soon until it calmed down and was safe.

"It'll be days, maybe even weeks. This stretch doesn't get much attention as they focus on clearing the main streets in Whiskey Mountain and Fallen Oaks first. Until there's more developed out here, it'll continue to be a low priority like it always has been."

Her voice was calmer, and for once, she didn't look like she wanted to kill me, which was odd.

"I, um, I'm sorry. I didn't mean to keep you from getting out of here on time to make it home. I feel bad that you're stuck here too."

She shook her head, grabbed the bags, and headed back into the shop.

"I'm not stuck here," she said over her shoulder. "I live here."

"You live here?" I set the bags I was holding beside hers on the floor, out of the way.

"Yeah, there are rooms in the back that I converted from storage and office space to living space a few months ago."

"Well, good, now I don't feel as bad about you not being able to get home because of me. Though I am sorry that you're stuck with me for the foreseeable future."

She looked around the room, her eyes roaming the space as if she were looking for an answer to a question I didn't know.

"It's fine, but I don't have anywhere for you to stay. The rooms in the back aren't very big, but we can try to figure something out. Follow me."

She didn't smile as she took off walking, expecting me to follow her.

I knew this was unplanned and hated that I had put her on the spot to share her space with Rosco and me, but it wasn't like I had any other choice. There was no way I could find my truck right now, let alone drive it. And even if I could find it, we would freeze to death if we tried to use it for shelter until the storm passed. Staying with Ramona was the only option we had.

"This is the kitchen. There's food in the fridge that you can help yourself to and stuff in the cabinets. Just don't get into my Cool Ranch Doritos or Milk Duds," she warned, pointing a finger at me as she stood behind one of the folding chairs scattered around the small circular table. "I stocked up on coffee today, so there should be plenty to get us through until the roads are cleared."

"Don't worry, I'm not a coffee drinker. It's all yours. And I promise I won't touch your snacks."

She eyed me suspiciously before giving me a tour of the rest of the space. There was a small room with a desk that she said was currently being used as her office and then a much larger room that she had converted into a bedroom.

"I can see if I have a sleeping bag," she offered as she rummaged through the walk-in closet.

There was a lot happening in the bedroom, but surprisingly, it didn't feel cramped or cluttered. A queen-sized bed sat along one wall with a dresser across from it and a TV mounted above. There was a nightstand on one side of the bed, and a surprisingly elaborate cat tower on the other, which I assumed belonged to the cat sprawled out on the navy floral comforter.

Along the wall with the window was a dog bed on the floor and a glass enclosure tucked into the corner. I couldn't tell whether it was a snake or a lizard inside, but whatever it was looked like it relied on plenty of heat, given the setup she had on top. I squinted to try to see it but was distracted by the sounds of her groaning from the closet as she moved stuff around.

"Sorry, I don't know where I put the damn thing," she called from inside it. "I was in a rush to get moved in, and things got thrown wherever they would fit."

"You don't have to worry about finding one," I said, making sure my voice carried across the room to her.

"I don't have anything else to offer if not." She came out and planted her hands on her hips, looking hotter than hell, which made it hard for me to think straight.

"We could share the bed," I suggested, wondering if there was anything in here she could shank me with. "It looks big enough to fit both of us, plus the cat." I pointed to where it had rolled over and stretched out further.

Her eyebrows rose into her hairline.

"What?"

"Share the bed," I repeated, patting the edge of it. "It's plenty big enough for both of us."

"You want me to share *my* bed with *you*?"

"I don't see why not. There aren't any other options since we're stuck together until this storm passes, and you owe me."

I shoved my hands into my pockets and leaned against the bedpost while I watched the features on her face change.

"I owe you? For what?"

"Pretending to be your boyfriend. If I hadn't spent time putting on that charade for your ex, I would have had time to get to a pet store before the storm rolled in and wouldn't be stranded here with you."

Her eyes narrowed further as she chewed her bottom lip angrily.

"Bullshit."

"It's true." I shrugged and pushed off the bedpost, stepping toward her until we were almost toe to toe. "If I wasn't so busy making out with you on aisle 5, I would have gotten everything done and avoided all of this."

"I'm the only pet store in town. You wouldn't have gotten anything done until I got home."

"Maybe. But I don't think that's what you're really upset about."

"90% of what you say upsets me."

She was putting the wall up again and trying to push me away, but I didn't care because she was hot as fuck when she was like this.

"Is that so?"

"Yes."

"Then why did you kiss me earlier?"

"I didn't. You kissed me, remember?"

"You kissed me back."

"I was faking it. Making sure it looked believable."

"Na," I said, leaning closer to her so my breath brushed against her temple as I spoke softly in her ear. "I felt the way you kissed me and how your body reacted to me. That wasn't faking."

"Apparently, you don't know a damn thing about me." Her words were laced with anger, but I could feel her body pulling into mine. There was a gravitational force that neither of us could deny, even if we wanted to.

"I think you don't want me in your bed because you don't trust yourself next to me."

"Oh, please," she scoffed, refusing to look at me.

"Then what's the real problem?"

"The real problem is that it isn't big enough because Daisy sleeps there, too."

"Who's Daisy?" I asked, wondering if some guy was hanging out that I hadn't seen when she'd given me the tour. There were a few rooms that we passed but didn't go into, so it wouldn't be totally inconceivable.

I waited for her to tell me, but her cell phone started ringing instead. She snapped out of whatever trance she was in, stormed down the hall, and slammed the bathroom door after she retreated inside, leaving me alone in her bedroom.

Seven

Ramona

"Hey," I whispered, tucking myself into the corner of the bathroom so Preston couldn't hear me. Not that I imagined him to be standing outside, lurking by the restroom. But then again, I didn't know the guy, so who knew what he was into?

"Hey," Maggie answered cheerfully. "Just checking to make sure you're okay and that you were able to get what you needed before the storm hit. Are you home and safe?"

"Yeah, I'm fine," I muttered, chewing my nail as I tried to figure out how to get rid of Preston, even though it wasn't a realistic possibility right now.

"What's wrong?"

"Preston's here," I whispered, trying to keep my freak out to a minimum.

"Where?"

"At Cool Cats."

"Why?"

"He came by to get supplies for his dog, and now he's stranded here because of the stupid storm."

"He has a dog? Aww, what kind?"

"Maggie!" I exclaimed, gripping the phone tighter. "Can you focus, please?"

"I am, but I don't see what the problem is." She laughed and I hated how light-hearted she was about this right now. Things were about to explode around me, and my best friend didn't even care.

"The problem is that he is stuck here—at Cool Cats. I have to share a space with him for who knows how long!"

"You're a grown woman, Ramona. I think you can bottle up your hostility toward him for a few days and figure out how to be around him without trying to murder him."

"I don't know," I sighed heavily. "I don't think I can handle him being that close to me 24/7 for days—maybe weeks."

"Why not?"

"Because—he makes me feel all…" I couldn't bring myself to finish the sentence.

"Horny like you want to ride the hard-cock express?" she offered, giggling on the other side.

"Maggie!"

"Oh, how the tables have turned," she said with a laugh. "Wasn't that the same thing you told me a while ago?"

"Yes, but it's only funny when it's about someone other than me. Plus, you totally wanted to board Owen's hard-cock express."

"Why are you being so weird about this? You've had Dylan stay over with you a few times since you moved into Cool Cats. Why is it so different to let Preston stay there for a few days?"

Because I didn't kiss Dylan, nor did I fantasize about what he might do to me if we shared a bed.

"It's just different, that's all."

"Why?"

She really wasn't going to let go of this, and I knew I would eventually tell her about it anyway.

"Because he kissed me."

"What?!"

I pulled the phone away as she shrieked in my ear.

"Do you have to be so loud?"

"You kissed Preston and expected me to be quiet about it?"

"Correction—I didn't kiss him. He kissed me."

"I'm so confused," Maggie said.

You and me both, my friend.

"It was all part of the ruse in making Daniel think we were together."

"Daniel? How does he fit into this?"

I exhaled heavily and then decided to spill all of it so she could get caught up and I could figure out how to get out of this shit show I'd gotten myself into.

"I was at Super Seven getting what I needed for the storm and ran into Preston on the wine aisle. I was trying to get a bottle from the bottom shelf when Daniel popped up out of thin air. I very quietly threatened to rearrange Preston's organs with broken glass if he didn't agree to pretend to be my boyfriend. He obliged and took the assignment a little too literally."

"So he just kissed you right there, in the middle of the wine aisle?"

"No, he kissed me a few aisles over because he knew Daniel was waiting to talk to me."

"Well, it sounds like it was just a simple kiss, and you both knew what you were doing. Why is it stressing you out so much?"

"Because," I exhaled. "It wasn't *just* the kiss. It was the way his fingers felt against my skin and the way he slapped my ass. Those were feelings that I've never felt before, and I can't process what it is with him constantly in my space, making me feel all… I don't even know what the word is."

"Horny. The word is horny, Ramona."

"Shut up. No, it isn't."

"You can deny it all you want to, but you know I'm right. He sparked something deep inside you, and while you'd love to act like you still hate him, you really want him to fuck your brains out."

I chewed the inside of my lip while I studied my reflection in the mirror. Was that true? Did I want him to fuck my brains out?

I mean, I wouldn't say no if he asked because I was super intrigued to see what else he could do, given he already had me on edge, and yet he'd barely touched me.

"Are you still there?" Maggie asked.

"Yeah, sorry. I was just thinking."

"About fucking Preston? I figured."

"Ugh, you're the worst," I joked.

"I know. But you love me anyway."

"Most days."

"Every day."

"Eh."

"Go get laid so I can have my happy best friend back. This one has been super cranky for months now, and that vibrating rose isn't doing the trick anymore."

"I'm not going to go get laid. Trust me, that's the last thing that will be happening between us. Just because you have Owen to satisfy those needs doesn't mean the rest of us are that lucky."

"If you say so," she sing-songed.

"I better get going. I don't know where he's at or what he's doing, so I need to make sure he doesn't let Daisy out."

"Alright, well, if you need anything, call me. Given how strong the wind is, I'm sure we'll lose power soon. Don't forget to charge your phone before then."

"Will do. Call if you need anything too."

I hung up and shoved my phone in my pocket before bracing myself against the sink. My cheeks were flushed, and I couldn't shake the thought of Preston fucking me, which only enhanced the redness. I grabbed my makeup bag, brushed some powder on my face, and prayed for the best.

The truth was that I wasn't ready to deal with someone else being in my space right now—regardless of who it was. Running into Daniel had been unexpected, and even though we'd been broken up for months, I hadn't seen him more than a few times since then. Even though Whiskey Mountain was a small town, he stayed inside most days, playing video games and living off the unemployment money he was getting after he got laid off shortly after we broke up.

I technically lived in Fallen Oaks now and only went to Whiskey Mountain to see Maggie and Dylan. We went to restaurants that I knew Daniel hated, just to avoid running into him. I also spent a lot of time at Spill The Beans, knowing that the likelihood of him walking in for a cup of coffee was zilch since he preferred beer most days.

But seeing him at the store today made me feel off, and I couldn't put my finger on why. Did I still want to be with him? No. But at the same time, I hated his smug attitude about me not being able to do this on my own. Sure, I'd moved in with him shortly after we became a couple, but it wasn't like he had purchased the house of his dreams and we were building our lives together. He had inherited an old, beat-up, single-story house that his grandpa left him when he died.

It was up to Daniel to fix it up and make it into what he wanted, but he lacked both the determination and desire to do anything with it. I'd made several recommendations on projects we could do together, but each one was brushed off and dismissed because it was *his family's house*.

I knew that Daniel wasn't struggling to make ends meet right now, given that he didn't have a mortgage and his parents had given him a brand-new truck when he graduated. The truck had been used and abused over the years, but he didn't have a payment on that either. His unemployment money would be enough to support his weekly groceries and beer, allowing him to live the life of his dreams: staying home all day, drinking beer, and playing video games until he was drunk by dinner time.

I fixed the lopsided bun on top of my head, squared my shoulders, and lied to myself about how I could spend the next few days with Preston without feeling something toward him.

Whether that feeling was horny or murderous, I wasn't sure.

Eight

Preston

I was sitting on the floor, trying to get Rosco to sit, when Ramona walked in. I didn't want to intrude, even though we would be staying here for a little while. I knew that it was as much of a shock to her as it was to me, and the last thing I wanted to do was make her uncomfortable.

"Sit," I commanded, holding a sausage-shaped treat in one hand while using the other to push Rosco's butt down.

His tail wagged excitedly as he lunged for it and almost snatched it from my grip.

"You need to teach him hand signals," Ramona said, grabbing the bag of treats from the floor beside me. "If you're going to train him to be obedient, you should be able to give him a sign without speaking and have him do what you're asking. That means that you'll also need to take him to public places and continue his training in those environments."

She stood in front of him, held her hand out in front of her with her palm facing up, and then raised it in an upward motion toward her shoulder while saying sit.

I was about to laugh and tell her *good luck, he doesn't know how to do that*, but as if some magical being had possessed him, he fucking did as she asked and plopped his ass on the linoleum floor.

"What the actual fuck?" I muttered, scrubbing a hand down my face. "I've been working with him for fifteen minutes and then you come out and he does it on the first try?"

"Most likely, he was already being taught in his previous home."

"I doubt it. My mom barely wanted to take the time to teach me and my brother when we were growing up. I can't imagine her doing it with a dog."

"No," she laughed, the sound surprisingly pleasant to my ears because I didn't hear it often enough from her. "I meant the people she bought him from. I know a few people in Whiskey Mountain who do dog training, and I believe Laurelyn mentioned something about her labradoodle having puppies soon. I'm guessing that's where your mom got him, and if I know Laurelyn, she was training them as early as she could."

"You can train dogs that young?"

She shrugged and repeated the command, smiling when he sat for another treat.

"Sometimes. Most dogs can start learning commands around 8 weeks, but exposing them to it early doesn't hurt. As long as you keep their training brief—maybe 5 minutes at most, and give positive reinforcement at the end, it's pretty easy."

"Easy for *you*," I teased, pushing up off the floor and wiping my hands on my jeans. "He hasn't been out since I left the house. Is there somewhere I can take him without worrying that you'll lock the door and leave us stranded in the blizzard?"

She pursed her lips, but I could see the hint of a smile playing on them.

"I would never leave Rosco outside to get stranded in a blizzard."

"Just Rosco? What about me?"

"Eh." She shrugged and waved for us to follow her down the hall.

She opened a door and stepped to the side, allowing us to enter first.

"Woah." It was the only thing I could get out because words couldn't describe the room we'd just walked into. "What is all of this?"

"This is Cool Cat's Dreamland," she said wistfully, closing the door. "I had this idea to open a pet daycare/play area for dogs. People could bring them in to hang out and burn off some energy while they went to work. Last year I started adding on to the existing structure and was able to design exactly what I wanted. The property sits on a large piece of land that my family owns, so it was easy to expand some without jumping through a bunch of hoops. Things were going great, but then my ex and I broke up, and I had to halt the project."

The room was massive, with kennels on one side of the walls, each with its own dog bed and food and water bowls. The floor was concrete, which Rosco enjoyed sniffing as we walked around and took everything in. A small patch of artificial grass was by a door that I assumed led outside, though I had no idea.

"He can go on the grass," Ramona said, pointing at it. "It's small enough that I can wash it in the shower, which is what I do for Daisy."

I nodded and led him over to it, where he promptly lifted his leg and relieved himself.

"Who's Daisy?" I asked, remembering her mentioning her earlier before her phone rang and she ran off.

"Daisy is this cute little girl," she replied, lifting a small dog out of a bed in one of the kennels.

She cuddled her in her arms against her chest and snuggled her as she yawned. Once she was awake and licking her face, she brought her over and sat her down on the grass next to Rosco.

As soon as I saw that Daisy was missing one of her back legs, I immediately pulled Rosco's leash to steer him away so he didn't hurt her.

"He's fine," she said, waving me off as she stood and watched the dogs together.

"I don't want Rosco to hurt her."

"Her best friend is a Weimaraner. She's fine."

"But…" I stuttered, wondering if she was aware that her dog only had three legs because she sure as hell didn't seem like it.

"She only has three legs?" she finished for me. "I know. It doesn't bother her at all. When I first got Daisy, it was after she had been hit by a car and her back leg was amputated. Her owner didn't want the responsibility of caring for her and doing rehab, so I took her in. Believe it or not, I don't think she even realizes that she's missing that leg anymore. She's gotten so used to going about without it."

"How long ago did it happen?"

"Two years."

"Wow. You've done a great job rehabbing her."

"Thank you." She looked up at me from under her dark lashes. "It helped that it was her hind leg instead of one of her front legs since that's where most of their body weight is concentrated. Plus, she's a small dog, so it wasn't as problematic for her. I bring her in here a few times a day and make her play when I can't take her for walks due to the weather."

"That's really cool. If I lived close by, I would love a place like this to take Rosco during the day to work off some of his energy."

"It's not that far," she said, frowning.

"Not right now, but when I go home it will be."

"To Fallen Oaks?"

It was my turn to frown.

"No, to Atlanta."

Her eyebrows rose as if she didn't expect me to say that.

"Oh. Sorry, I guess I just assumed that you were still in Fallen Oaks with your family."

"I moved to Atlanta a year ago after I got my master's degree. Been there ever since."

"What is your degree in?" she asked, neither of us looking at each other as we watched the dogs walk around and take turns sniffing each other.

"Computer science."

Her head whipped up as she looked at me with a shocked expression.

"So that's why you asked about my computer!"

It wasn't a question but more of a realization.

I nodded and rocked back on my heels.

"Do you really think you can fix it?"

"I don't know. First, I would have to look at it to see what the problem is."

"Okay. How much do you charge because I will gladly pay whatever it is if you can make that stupid black screen stop appearing. It's killing me," she groaned.

"I don't want your money," I replied, rubbing my lips together.

Her eyes scanned my face, and her cheeks turned the faintest shade of red as if she was imagining what I might want.

"Okay…" She turned to face me and schooled her features. "What do you want instead?"

"I want to share your bed."

50

Nine

Ramona

"Is this Vin Diesel on your screensaver?" Preston asked, looking up at me as I popped a Cool Ranch Dorito into my mouth.

I nodded and hoped he couldn't see the blush on my cheeks with the fluorescent lights in the kitchen. It was the only space big enough for us to sit and eat dinner without hanging out in the shop. Rosco was in the play yard with Daisy, even though it took a lot of convincing for Preston to trust that his dog wouldn't eat mine. Once I showed him the cameras I had set up, he finally relaxed and agreed to come and have dinner.

"Do I want to know why you have yourself photoshopped on Michelle Rodriguez's body?"

"Because I want to be Letty," I laughed, covering my mouth so chip crumbs didn't shoot out.

He pulled his brows together and frowned.

"You know… Letty? Dom's girlfriend?"

Nothing. Just a blank stare as if I were speaking a foreign language.

I grabbed my phone from the table and pulled up the original image from the movie where she was sitting on his lap in the garage. I turned it to face him, trying not to laugh when he squinted his eyes and leaned closer to see it.

"No clue who that is."

"What?! That's Dom Toretto and Letty from *The Fast and The Furious*!"

"Never seen it."

My eyes bulged as I looked at him and then back to my phone.

"How could you have *not* seen it? It's a classic!"

"*Rocky. Gone In Sixty Seconds. Terminator. Gladiator.*"

I scrunched my nose and set my phone back down on the table before grabbing another chip out of the bag.

"What are you listing? Popular movies in retirement homes?"

He narrowed his eyes at me briefly before focusing on my laptop again.

"No. *Those* are classics."

"Maybe if you're super old. How old are you anyway?"

"Old enough to appreciate the true classics."

"Agree to disagree," I sighed, the crunch of the chips loud in my ears as I chewed. "Dom was hotter than any of those guys."

"I don't check men out, so I guess I'll have to go with whatever you say."

"You can't tell me that Letty isn't hot," I countered, grabbing my phone again. "Just look at her!"

"So you pasted your face on her body so you could be like her or so you could have her man?"

I shrugged sheepishly, hating that he was getting a little too close to the truth.

"Both, I guess."

"Do you have leather pants?"

"No, I don't. Why?"

"Because if you did, I could have you put them on and then decide who looks hotter in them. The girl in front of me that I could take them off of, or some girl on the internet that I could care less about."

I swallowed hard, thankful that the chip I'd eaten had fully passed down my throat before it could get lodged in it with how dry it suddenly was.

I got up and grabbed a glass from the cabinet, filling it with ice-cold water from the fridge. Preston was flirting with me—there was no doubt about that. The real question was why…

The cold liquid felt good as I chugged it like I was stranded on a deserted island. He lifted his sandwich to his lips, took a bite, then set it down before wiping the crumbs away with his thumb. The whole thing felt oddly erotic to watch, which was weird given that he was making a plain turkey and cheese sandwich look so arousing.

I pressed the glass against the bar and refilled it, barely paying enough attention to move it before it spilled over. I continued to watch him as he ate, completely entranced by how sexy it all looked. That was one fucking lucky sandwich.

But then again, it had nothing to do with the sandwich. He could be eating a piece of celery and it would have the same effect on me. Maybe deep down, I wanted to be the celery. We weren't that different anyway, both of us long and slender and, as of right now, packed full of water.

I set the glass down with a heavy thud on the counter, grabbing Preston's attention for a few seconds before he returned to fixing my computer. My stomach felt sloshy, and I knew that it was because I had just drunk my weight in water.

"So, I think I figured out—"

The lights flickered as the wind howled outside. They had been doing so for about half an hour and I was just waiting for the power to finally go out.

"Well, I was going to say that I think I figured out what's wrong with your computer," Preston said. "But given that I don't know how much longer we'll have power, I don't want to risk it starting on it right now."

As if right on cue, there was a loud thud outside, and then everything around us went pitch black.

Ten

Preston

"It looks like a tree fell against the wall right by the door. It must have gotten knocked down by the wind," I said, coming inside and shaking the snow from my hair. Ramona had grabbed a few candles and had given me a flashlight when I offered to go check to see what had happened. I didn't get far before spotting the fallen tree and knew that was the source of the noise. The power going out at the same time was just a coincidence but not a surprise, given how long the lights had been flickering before it finally cut out.

"Was there any damage?" she asked, sitting in the same spot in the kitchen where I had left her.

"Not that I could tell, but then again, I could barely see the tree. The snow hasn't let up and I can't see more than a few inches in front of me."

"It's going to get cold in here soon," she said, getting up and taking her plate to the sink. "We should probably call it a night and get some sleep. Maybe the power will be back when we wake up."

"Okay."

We still hadn't discussed where I would sleep tonight or what to do with Rosco. He was a puppy, and this was technically our first night together, so I had no clue what to expect from him. While I had teased her about us sharing her bed, I didn't actually mean it and didn't want to make her uncomfortable.

"There's extra space on the floor in my room if you want to put Rosco's bed there. If not, I have a big crate in the play yard that we can bring inside for him. I think it's big enough to stuff his bed in. It's up to you and whatever you think he'll do better in."

"Honestly, I have no idea. I just got him today, so I don't know what he's used to sleeping in or how he'll do."

I hated that I couldn't see her face in the dim light from the candle.

"Maybe it's better to crate him then. That way, he'll have his bed but can't wander or pace if he gets anxious. We can add a blanket or two to make sure he has a place to hide if he wants to."

"Sounds good. If you tell me where it is, I can get him set up. Just point me in the direction of where you want us."

"Okay, I'll go with you to get it."

I followed her to the playroom and held the flashlight above her head to light the way.

"You can grab that one," she said, pointing to the large one in the corner. "It's not as heavy as it looks. I carry it by myself all the time."

"Is that going to fit in your room?" I asked, taking in how large it was.

She turned to face me, her nose scrunched up.

"Yeah, maybe not. I forgot how big it was."

"I thought you said you carry it by yourself all the time?" I teased, shining the light at her like a cop would.

"I do," she laughed. "But it's just around in here. I never take it out of this room unless I have to."

I patted Rosco's head as we stared at the crate and tried to figure out how to move it to her room.

"I don't think it's going to fit in your room," I said.

"Yeah, looking at it now, I don't think so either."

"It's pretty warm in here. I think he might be okay to stay in here tonight if you're okay with it?"

She looked around and then looked at me.

"I don't want Rosco to sleep in here alone. What if he gets scared or lonely?"

"He's a dog. I think he'll be just fine. It's not like we're throwing him outside and making him sleep in the snow."

"No, but he's just a baby. He's probably used to sleeping in the same bed with his mom and siblings. It's hard for dogs to be separated from their pack and then to force them into an environment where they don't know what's going on—"

"Umm, Ramona?" I interrupted, looking down into one of the kennels beside us.

"What? I know what I'm talking about. He's going to whine and cry all night. There's no way we can leave him alone. He needs a companion to feel safe."

"Like this one?"

I shone the flashlight into the crate to show her Rosco curled up in the bed with Daisy, snuggled up against each other.

"Oh my God!" she squealed, taking the flashlight from me and pointing it closer to get a better look. "Would you look at that?"

Daisy looked up at us, yawned, and then rested her head on Rosco's leg as she curled up between his legs. It was like he was the big spoon, and she was the little one.

"I've never seen Daisy act like that with another dog before. I think she loves him!"

"It sure looks like it."

"Well, I guess that problem is settled then. This room is well insulated, as that was my top priority, given how cold it gets here during the winter. On top of that, they have each other's body heat to stay warm and chose the fleece-lined bed. I think they're good."

"Alright, if you want to show me where you want me to sleep, I'll get out of your hair."

She whipped around, almost crashing into me as the light danced wildly between us. I grabbed the flashlight, holding it steady as my hand brushed against hers. I could feel the change in her the same way I had the other times we touched.

Her breathing quickened, the sound almost deafening in the room aside from my racing heartbeat.

"You can sleep in my room," she breathed out.

I couldn't help but pick up on something hidden in her words, probably because she didn't speak them with sarcasm like she usually did. There was a vulnerability there, one that I was eager to explore.

"You don't have to let me sleep in your bed, Ramona. I was just giving you a hard time."

"I can't remember the last time I had something hard."

"What?" I asked, not sure that I heard her correctly.

A slight gasp escaped her lips when she realized what she said. I felt my cheeks burn from the grin spreading across my face as I rocked back on my heels.

"What?" she repeated nervously, acting like she hadn't said what she had just said.

"Oh, nothing. You were just telling me how you haven't had anything hard in a long time, and I was about to ask if you wanted me to remedy that tonight," I teased, knowing it would rile her up as she denied it.

She stood there for a few minutes in stunned silence. Not that I was complaining because at least she wasn't threatening me. I placed my hand on her lower back and spun her around, guiding her out of the play yard and into the hallway leading to her bedroom. She didn't say anything the entire time. No snarky comebacks or remarks about how she would rather do anything *but me*, and I couldn't help but wonder if maybe my dirty mouth broke Ramona.

Eleven

Ramona

I can't remember the last time I had something hard.

Why the fuck did I say that?! Just because I had twisted Preston's words when he said he was giving me a hard time didn't mean that I wanted him to know that I was fantasizing about just how *hard* of a time he could give me.

Maybe I was lacking oxygen, and that's why I couldn't think straight right now. Was that a thing—a power outage related oxygen shortage? Because I was pretty sure that was what we were dealing with.

I allowed him to guide me back to my bedroom, unsure of what to do from there. I couldn't in good conscious give him a blanket and tell him to go find somewhere to sleep, but I also couldn't trust myself to sleep in the same bed next to him and keep my hands to myself. Since Daisy was now sleeping in the play yard with Rosco, that meant she wouldn't be crawling out of her bed to lick his face if he slept on the floor, but then again, I couldn't imagine asking him to sleep on the floor. Probably because deep down, I wanted him in my bed, even if I had been trying to convince him—and myself—that I didn't.

I had no idea what had gotten into me—it sure as hell wasn't Preston, but that was beside the point. Something about him made me feel different than anyone else ever had. It was like he had this magic spell over me, and I couldn't escape if I tried.

"So, about that enclosure in the corner," Preston said, shining the flashlight at it. "Is there anything in there?"

"Yes, that's Louie's home."

"And Louie is?"

We walked over to the cage together, and I peered in, trying to find him. He was good at camouflaging himself, to begin with, but with very little light, it made it even more difficult to spot him.

"He's my veiled chameleon." I pointed to the hanging branch toward the back, where he was hiding behind some leaves and fake plants. It was his favorite spot and close to the heat lamp, so I wasn't surprised to find him there.

Preston leaned in, brushing my arm in the process and sending a waft of his cologne into the air in front of me. I sucked in a deep breath, trying to keep my composure instead of jumping his bones as my legs tried to part for him involuntarily.

"So, what do we need to do for this little guy since there's no power for his heat lamp?"

I bet Preston doesn't have a little guy. I bet it's big and thick and can show a girl a good time.

I shook my head, trying to clear the fog so I could answer him.

"He should be fine for tonight. I cranked the heater up earlier in anticipation of the power going out so that when the temperature drops in here, it'll level out around the normal temperature. I also have some reptile heating pads in the store that I can use tomorrow if the power isn't back. For now, he's good. I sprayed his plants earlier so he has plenty of humidity, and he can go a little while without the UV light."

I reached around, trying not to touch him, and grabbed a blanket from beneath the cage on the shelf I used to store supplies.

"I also have this blanket that I wrap around the cage to keep some heat inside since it's right by the window. Thankfully the winters here are pretty predictable, so this isn't our first rodeo."

I lifted it to show him but was surprised when he grabbed the other end and helped me put it on.

"Alright, that should do it," I said, turning around and smacking right into his rock-hard chest.

Fuck. Me. Is everything about him hard?

His fingers lightly tickled my skin as they wrapped around me and held me in place.

I wanted to look up and ask him what he was doing. Demand that he stop whatever this game was that he was playing, but I couldn't. My mouth refused to work because my brain refused to generate the words it needed to do so. I had spent so long being angry and frustrated with him for existing, and now I was like a dog in heat and wanted nothing *but* Preston to touch me.

"Are you okay?" he asked, his voice low as his fingers trailed lightly over my skin.

While it was in the negative digits outside, I had been roasting from cranking the heater up and had stripped off the flannel shirt earlier, leaving me in just a tank top. This left easy access for him to leave goosebumps along my bare skin from his touch, sending me even further up the wall with desire.

"Yeah. I'm fine. We should sleep together."

My heart raced so fast that I could barely hear my thoughts past the rush of blood passing through my ears as my blood pressure skyrocketed.

Did I just ask him to sleep with me?

"Um, I mean. We should both sleep. At the same time. Not like together, together. I didn't mean it that way. Just in the same bed because the floor is hard. Not as hard as you. Or rather, how your chest was when I touched it a few minutes ago. That was hard. But I think everything about you is hard. I mean, I'm not insinuating that your cock is hard, too—shit! I mean, I hope it is. Not right now, because that might be weird. But in general. Like you know, when you're aroused? Fuck. Now it sounds like I think you can't get hard. I didn't mean it that way; I just meant that maybe you are hard when you want to be and that I'm not insinuating that you have erectile dysfunction or anything. I mean—"

"Ramona?"

"Yeah?"

"Stop talking."

I took a deep breath and held it to keep myself from rambling on again. I was actively aware that I was holding it so I didn't pass out because I didn't need to add any more humiliation to the mix tonight. The last thing I wanted to be was like one of those girls in the romance novels I read where they *finally let out the breath they didn't realize they were holding*. Who does that?

I felt the heat flame my cheeks as he stood in front of me, his fingers burning into my skin that was already on fire from humiliation. I had just gone on and on about Preston and whether or not he could get an erection. I knew I had suspicions earlier about oxygen deprivation related to power outages, but now I knew for sure that it had to be true. What else could explain the total moron that I had turned into since then?

"Which side do you prefer?" he asked, catching me off guard.

I tilted my head and studied his face, hoping it would give me a clue about what he was talking about. Was he asking which side I preferred to be fucked on? I was used to just lying on my back and faking it, so I didn't have much of a preference on sides. However, I was definitely curious about it now.

"Are you sure you're okay?" he asked again, this time lifting my chin with his fingers to bring my eyes back to his.

Something snapped inside of me, and without thinking, I reached up and wrapped my arms around his neck, pulling him into me for a kiss.

My lips roamed over his eagerly, the kiss deepening as he grabbed the back of my neck and held me there while he pressed harder against mine. I moaned into it, my body betraying me as I pulled myself up and wrapped my legs around his waist as I felt the ache start between my thighs. This man was pure fire and I wanted to feel his heat. Okay—cock. I wanted to feel his cock.

His big, strong hands slipped down, grazing my back before grabbing handfuls of ass and squeezing. I arched into his touch, desperate for more. My hips rocked against him, and I heard a low growl escape his throat as I brushed against his erection.

It was massive and impressive—just like I imagined it would be. How he used it was the more important question, but given that his hands and lips seemed to be experts in the pleasure department, I didn't have to worry that his cock would be disappointing.

Suddenly, he pulled away, breaking the kiss and leaving both of us panting.

"Are you sure you want to do this?" he asked, keeping his head away so I couldn't kiss him again without answering first.

"Yes. I do. Let's go." I rocked harder against him, practically trying to dry hump him if he would let me.

He chuckled and lowered me back to the floor.

"What's wrong?" I asked, not too proud to hide the disappointment in my voice. "Is it the whole hard thing I said a few minutes ago? Because I was totally wrong about that. Obviously." I pointed to the bulge in his jeans.

"No," he laughed. "But I'm glad I was able to prove your hypothesis."

Hypothesis? What the fuck was that? I was too horny right now for logical thoughts or big words.

I shook my head.

"Okay, then what's the problem?"

"I don't know." He sighed and scrubbed a hand down his face. "I guess it's that I don't want to rush into something that you might regret when you're thinking clearly."

"Why would I regret it?" I rushed out a little too eagerly.

If he knew how long it had been since I had sex with someone who was rocking as hard of a cock as he was through his jeans, he wouldn't worry about me having any regrets.

"Because you've been trying to shoot lasers out of your eyes and into my head since I met you. You've threatened to kill me several times and now you're practically trying to ride me through my jeans."

I inhaled deeply and took a step back, hoping to find some air that wasn't contaminated with his scent. Maybe it wasn't an oxygen-related power outage at all. Perhaps I was just stupid around him because he somehow sucked all the brain cells out of my head without trying.

"So?"

"So? I don't know, Ramona. I guess maybe I'm just not sure whether to trust that you won't stab me with something as you climax. I don't know where this change came from— not that I don't like it. I mean, it's better than worrying about you plotting my gruesome murder and feeding me to the wild animals outside. But this is the first time you've been friendly to me since I set foot in Whiskey Mountain, so I don't know where it's coming from."

"There aren't any wild animals to worry about." I rolled my eyes though he couldn't see.

I didn't want to get into the reasons why I was suddenly being nice to him because it meant that I would have to stop and process it myself, and I wasn't in the mood to do that. There was something about Preston that made me feel different than anyone had ever made me feel before, and I was worried that if I didn't stop and act on this right here, right now, then it would disappear just as quickly as it came about.

"Pretty sure I heard some howling when I went to check on the noise," he added to fill the silence between us.

I shrugged my shoulders though I wasn't sure he could see it.

"I just think that we shouldn't rush into this." His voice was soft, but his words felt like they cut through me with a knife.

I didn't date much growing up and got with Daniel our senior year in high school. We didn't make it official until a year later, but we were still a thing. He was the only long-term relationship I've ever had, and aside from a few random hook ups after we broke up, I didn't know what it felt like to be with anyone but him.

Daniel wasn't perfect, but when we first started dating, he looked at me like I hung the moon and stars. He gave me everything I could ever ask for before things began to decline. Even then, feeling the change between us as we drifted apart didn't hurt nearly as bad as getting rejected by Preston.

68

Twelve

Preston

To say that Ramona was pissed off would be an understatement. It wasn't just the silent treatment she gave me last night when we went to bed or the pillow she shoved in my face because she "couldn't see where my head was," AKA she didn't *mean to* try to smother me. It was the way I could feel her shooting those daggers through my head again in the dead of night and how I relied on her snoring to know that she wasn't getting ready to shank me in my sleep.

I slept like shit—probably because I was trying to do it with one eye open. Or maybe it was because it was hard for me to sleep at night in general. Insomnia always crept up on me, and last night was no different. I finally decided to stop fighting it and got up for the day around five in the morning.

The power was still out, and I didn't want to waste what battery I had left on my cell phone by playing on it, so I went into the store and hung out until Ramona woke up. I had noticed her stocking the shelves yesterday when I first got there and saw that there were still a few boxes she hadn't gotten to. Determined to make myself helpful and not like the villain she thought I was, I started unpacking them and filled the shelves.

I was in the groove, slinging boxes of fish food onto the display next to the fish tanks, belting out my rendition of All Out of Love by Air Supply, when she walked in and scared the shit out of me.

"Those don't go there," she said, pointing to the boxes I had thrown in the air, landing on the floor between us.

"Sorry. You startled me." I bent down and started gathering them while she stood over me, watching.

"Well, I wasn't expecting to hear karaoke in the store this early in the morning. Is that one of the songs on the playlist at the retirement home? Do they play it between showings of Rocky and Gladiator?" she teased. Or at least I thought she was teasing. The way her hazel eyes darkened made me suddenly unsure.

"Laugh all you want, but Air Supply is a legendary band, and All Out of Love hit the number two spot on the Billboard Hot 100 in February 1980. In addition, they've had 7 other songs make the list as well. It's a classic, just like the movies."

"You do realize that we're not in the 80s, right? Were you even born in the 80s, or do you just have some old man spirit trapped in your body?"

"No, I wasn't born in the 80s, but my parents taught me to appreciate music from across many decades and to broaden my horizons. Just because something is old doesn't mean that it loses its value. It's called being open-minded."

"There's also nothing wrong with appreciating things from *this* decade," she remarked, redoing the boxes of food I had already put on the shelf.

"You're right. Unfortunately, I don't care for much of the so-called music from this decade. I'd much rather listen to something with soul and meaning. If music from this decade contained even an *ounce* of that, I would be willing to give it a try."

She shook her head but said nothing as her shoulders tightened. I was getting to her again without even trying.

"So, do you have anything else you need unpacked?" I

asked, trying to change the subject.

"I have more boxes in the back that I've been meaning to go through, but you don't have to do that."

"I don't mind, really. I like staying busy, and it's not like I have anywhere to go."

She narrowed her eyes at me and placed her hands firmly on her hips.

"Why are you being nice?"

"I'm not. I'm bored and cold. Moving around keeps my blood flowing and helps me stay warm. Plus, it helps pass the time. So, if you need help with stuff, stop being stubborn and let me do it."

"I'm not starting on anything until I've had breakfast. You can come eat or stay here and freeze your balls off. It's up to you, but this is the coldest room in the building."

I pursed my lips and debated whether to join her or not. She seemed just as grumpy as she was last night when we went to bed, and I wasn't sure what it would take to improve her mood. I mean, I had an idea, but I couldn't imagine that walking into the kitchen with my cock out was going to go over well, even if that's what she really wanted. Knowing my luck, she'd come at it with a butcher's knife, which was a risk I wasn't willing to take.

"Are you coming or not?" she asked over her shoulder as she turned on her heel and walked away.

Against my better judgment, I followed her.

Thirteen

Ramona

"There are bagels on the counter or some granola bars in the cabinet. Help yourself."

I reached up on my tiptoes and grabbed the box of Frosted Flakes cereal from the top shelf in the pantry. I wasn't big on breakfast and only ate it because I got super cranky when I skipped meals. While I preferred to eat cereal with milk, I didn't trust that the gallon I had in the fridge was still good since the power had been out for so long. It had been over twelve hours and it wouldn't be the first time that milk had given me a sour surprise, so I wasn't testing my luck today.

Preston grabbed a granola bar out of the box and then closed the cabinet while he stood there to eat it. I could tell he wasn't comfortable sitting at the table with me, and I couldn't blame him. I'd been a raging bitch since last night, but that's what being mortified did to me.

I couldn't remember the last time I'd made a move on a guy that wasn't reciprocated. Granted, he was into it at first, but he also ended it and ultimately rejected me. I thought that I would be more grown up and mature about how I would handle it *if* it ever happened to me, but I guess I didn't give myself credit for thinking I could land a guy like Preston in the first place.

"You're eating dry cereal?" he questioned, keeping from raising his eyebrows even though the judgment was still laced in his tone.

"I don't trust the milk."

"Why not eat something else? I can't imagine that it's that satisfying to eat dry cereal. It's gotta be all scratchy and hard to get down."

"Because I like cereal. If I like something, I eat it. I don't make a big deal about it or find stuff that I don't like as much just because it fits the situation."

He rubbed his lips together and then popped the last piece of granola bar into his mouth before tossing the wrapper into the trash.

I continued eating but hated that he was right. It wasn't satisfying at all, and my mouth was dry. Typically, I would wash it down with my morning coffee, but given that we didn't have power still, it wasn't like I could make any.

"This sucks," I muttered under my breath, pushing the container away from me.

"What does?"

"Nothing."

My mood was getting sourer by the minute, and I didn't want to keep making myself a bigger bitch than I already was.

"What sucks, Ramona?" he pressed, crossing an ankle over the other as he casually leaned against the counter.

"That the power is out. That I don't trust that the milk is still good. That I can't even make coffee. That it's fucking colder than a witch's tit in here."

His lips curled up at the last one.

"I can make you coffee," he offered.

I cocked my head and glared at him.

"And how exactly are you going to do that?" I asked, trying not to get my hopes up.

"Do you have a kettle?"

"Yeah…"

"Is your water heater gas or electric?"

"Gas, thank God. There's no way I could go days without a hot shower."

"Grab the kettle, and I'll start getting everything else ready."

He moved about the kitchen, looking at the basic coffee maker sitting on the counter like it was the most complicated thing he'd ever seen.

"I don't believe in buying expensive coffee makers when this works just fine," I said, handing the steel kettle to him.

"I agree. Basic is best." He took it and went to the sink, waiting a few seconds until the water was hot.

I was a sucker for super-hot showers and baths, so I kept the temperature set high which meant he would burn himself in a matter of seconds if he didn't remove his fingers from the stream.

Finally, he pulled away and lowered the kettle into the stream, filling it as the steam billowed from the top.

I stood back and watched as he added a few scoops of coffee grounds to the filter and then very slowly poured the hot water over them in a circular motion. It felt like a magic trick as the coffee machine gurgled to life and liquid gold began dripping into the carafe.

The smell filled the air, bringing a smile to my face as my spirits lifted. I knew that Preston was watching me and hated that he was the reason for my happiness.

"No fucking way! That's amazing!" I exclaimed, genuinely

impressed with his ability to make me coffee. "Thank you."

"It's not a big deal." He shrugged and poured the last bit of water in before setting the kettle on the trivet by the stove.

"How did you learn to do that?"

"Growing up, my parents took us camping a few times a year. They believe in using the resources you have available and taught my brother and me at an early age how to do a lot of things."

"Like making coffee during a power outage," I said with a smile.

"It's really quite simple. The only thing the machine does is heat the water before it spreads it over the coffee grounds. I just did the work for it."

"Well, I'm still impressed and very thankful for the coffee. It may not be a honey lavender latte from Spill The Beans, but it's definitely better than nothing."

"Glad I could help."

"Have you been to Spill The Beans? I know you said you don't drink coffee, but you're seriously missing out. I don't know what it is about that latte, but it just calms me down and makes me feel amazing."

He shook his head and smiled.

"No, I haven't been."

"You really should try it. It's amazing and magical."

"That's probably because lavender counteracts the negative effects of coffee. You get the energy jolt from the coffee without having the jittery side effects of the caffeine."

I pulled my head back in shock.

"Excuse me? There are no negative effects of coffee."

"Not true," he said, shaking his head and folding his arms over his chest. "Coffee is a stimulant, and depending on the amount consumed, it can induce anxiety, restlessness, insomnia, and even impact things like elevated heart rate and blood pressure. By adding lavender, you're slightly counteracting some of the negatives with the positive effects of it."

"Oh yeah? Like what?"

I knew I was in a losing battle, given that Preston seemed to know so much about everything, but part of me wanted to hear him talk about it. It was fascinating in a weird sort of way.

"Well, lavender contains a compound called linalool. It creates a soothing effect on the body when consumed in either tea or coffee. It also stimulates activity in certain areas of the brain, and the calming aroma helps it secrete serotonin while decreasing cortisol levels. When combined with coffee or tea, it allows the caffeine to provide the energy boost that you want while also giving you the soothing effect you desire."

The coffee was finally done, and the drip had stopped, so I pulled the carafe out and filled a cup for myself since Preston didn't drink coffee. I grabbed some powdered creamer and a few packets of sugar out of the cabinet and added them in, all while trying to come up with a witty comeback to what he had said.

"What are you? Some sort of walking, talking encyclopedia?" I asked, lifting the cup to my lips and taking a sip. He didn't reply. Instead, he just winked at me, pushed off the counter, and walked out of the kitchen, leaving me alone with the best stupid cup of coffee I'd had at home in a long time.

Fourteen

Preston

"I'm not usually this big of a bitch," Ramona commented randomly as we put away the empty boxes that were broken down and ready to be recycled once the roads opened again.

"Okay." I wasn't sure what to say to that.

Had she been grumpy with me? Yes. Had she threatened bodily harm recently? Also, yes. But did I think she was a bitch? No. There was something about her that I couldn't figure out, but deep down, I knew that this whole mean girl front was just that—a facade.

"I just wanted you to know that I haven't *always* been this way, and I feel bad for taking it out on you when you've been kind enough to help me stock the store and make coffee this morning."

"It's not a big deal. Like I said, I don't mind helping."

"Yeah, but you don't have to."

"What else am I going to do? I'm stuck here until the storm passes through and the roads are cleared. There's no electricity. I looked around but didn't see any books to read. It leaves me with nothing to do but help out in here, and honestly, I like it."

"You like stocking shelves and doing inventory?" she questioned, twisting her body to see me.

"I do. I like staying busy and being active. I hate just sitting around all day."

"But don't you sit all day at work doing computer stuff?"

"Every now and then. But I also get to work from home, and I have a standing desk, so I don't have to sit that long. I also have a full gym set up at my house in Atlanta."

As much as I enjoyed being close to my family, I missed having my own space back home. It was a small house with a minimalistic design. The walls were still the same dull white color they were when I bought it, and I hadn't taken the time to hang any pictures or art. I had a few essential pieces of furniture, but most of my focus was on the gym. That was where I had splurged and dedicated all my focus.

"Do you like working from home?"

I nodded because I never knew how to answer that question when people asked it. It felt rude to say that I much preferred the silent solitude of an empty house than to sit around and pretend to be engaged in boring small talk with people I didn't even like.

"It works well for me," I replied, leaving it at that.

"I never thought I would have the opportunity to work from home, but it turned out it just took dumping my boyfriend and ending up homeless for it to happen. That was the kick in the pants I needed to make the renovations I had been putting off here for so long." She laughed.

"Was that the guy at the store?"

She nodded, her face falling some before she turned away from me.

"That's him. Daniel."

"How long were you guys together?"

She sighed heavily before answering.

"We dated off and on throughout high school, mostly our

senior year. After graduation, we were still dating, but he didn't make it *official* until we moved in together. So, if you count from that point—which he always did—we were together for 3 years."

"When do you count from?"

She shrugged and sat down on a box we hadn't unpacked yet.

"I guess from the moment I thought he was my boyfriend in high school. We were one of those couples who were always on again, off again, that it was hard to tell if we were together or not. I stayed committed to him, even on our breaks, but he didn't do the same. I should have seen what he was doing then, but I put my blinders on because I had the *hottest* boy at Fallen Oaks High. But then again, so did a lot of other girls, and I just pretended that I didn't know about it."

"That sucks. I'm sorry."

"Don't be. It's all for the better. I'm past that part of my life and ready to move on."

"Are you, though?" I questioned, though the way she stood up and narrowed her eyes at me made me immediately reconsider.

"Why wouldn't I be?"

"I don't know. I guess it was just the way you reacted to running into him at the store. It seemed like you still cared about what he thought about you."

She stepped closer and pointed a finger at me.

"You don't have a clue what you're talking about. I'm over Daniel. Leaving him was the best thing I've ever done."

"Then why did you need a fake boyfriend?" I countered, stepping closer and closing the gap between us.

"Why does it matter?"

"Because it does. You can't say that you're over him and don't care what he thinks when you threatened to stab me if I didn't pretend to be your new boyfriend."

"It was a rash decision," she hissed out. "One that I later regretted."

"What part?"

"All of it?"

"Liar."

She pulled her head back, her nostrils flaring with anger.

"You're calling me a liar?"

"You bet your sweet ass I am. You didn't regret one second of it. Not the way I kissed you, and sure as hell not the way your body reacted when I touched your ass."

"I was caught off guard, and it made me all—"

"Horny?" I offered, placing my leg between hers as I pinned her against the wall.

"No," she bit out, her words strained with the lie.

"Okay," I said slowly, gently placing my hand on her hip and looking around before allowing myself to look into those dark hazel eyes. "If you regretted it so much, why did you kiss me last night and try to get me to sleep with you?"

She opened her mouth to speak but then snapped it shut.

"You want me as bad as I want you, Ramona. Don't try to deny it because it's written all over your body."

"It is not."

Her chest rose and fell heavily as she folded her arms over it.

"If I would have said yes last night, you wouldn't have

stopped me from doing all of the dirty things you've been thinking about me doing to you."

"But you didn't. You turned me down, and now you're humiliating me again by bringing it up. There, are you happy?"

My eyes locked onto hers, reading the emotions flickering across her face as she struggled to hide them.

"I turned you down because I didn't want you to do something you would regret. If you were some girl that I met under different circumstances, I might have agreed to it. But given that I know that you're fresh off a breakup and having seen how you reacted to seeing Daniel, I don't trust that you're doing it for the right reasons, and I don't want to be the thing you regret."

She let her head fall back and closed her eyes.

"I'm very attracted to you—just so we're clear on that," I added, making sure she didn't think that I wasn't. "I don't want to be the guy you use to get over your ex."

She stood there for a few minutes, not speaking, while my hand refused to move from her body. I could tell there was something she wanted to say, and I wanted to give her the space she needed so she could.

Finally, her eyes opened and caught mine.

"I've spent most of my life trying to be what everyone wanted me to be and always feeling like I'm failing. Not only with my parents but with Daniel, too. When we broke up, he got to keep everything, and I was the one who had to start over and figure out how to make it on my own. I didn't have help from anyone but my friends and I wasn't sure I could do it because I had never been on my own before. When I ran into Daniel at the store, I panicked. The last thing he had told me when we broke up was that I would never find anyone who would put up with and tolerate me like he did, so I wanted to prove him wrong. I wanted to show him I could find someone, and you just happened to be there."

"He sounds like a real asshole."

She lifted a shoulder and let it fall with a sigh.

"He didn't use to be. He was the perfect boyfriend when we first started dating. Always complimenting me and showering me with affection. Over the years, it slowed down, and I assumed it was just because we had gotten so used to each other. I tried to keep the spark alive and asked him to try new things with me. I worried he didn't find me attractive anymore, so I started working out and went on crazy diets to lose weight. But in the end, nothing I did was good enough."

I shook my head, not wanting to believe what I was hearing.

"When I kissed you last night, it wasn't because I'm some pathetic, lonely girl looking to jump into another relationship. I felt something with you that I've never felt before, and for the first time in a long time, I was excited about it. I wanted to explore whatever it was and see if maybe I wasn't dead inside after all. But I'm sorry if I made you uncomfortable. That wasn't my intention, and I shouldn't have been shitty to you about it when you said no."

"I'm not going to lie, Ramona. You did make me feel uncomfortable."

Her face fell as she hurried to look away so I couldn't see the hurt in her eyes.

"It was incredibly uncomfortable going to bed last night with blue balls and trying to sleep knowing that you were only a few inches away from me, wearing those thin silky sleep shorts that barely covered your ass."

The thought of her plump cheeks peeking out of them last night flashed through my head, sending a reminder straight to my cock. I lowered my hand from her hip and grabbed hers, dropping it to the bulge in my jeans.

"This is what you do to me, Ramona," I growled in her

ear. "You're far from pathetic, and I feel the same insane chemistry you're feeling. If you want to act on this and explore whatever it is, fine with me. But you need to know before we start anything that I'm not a relationship guy. I don't do commitment. Never have, never will."

"I don't want one either," she rushed out, pressing her hand harder against me.

"Good."

"Good."

"We're just two friends that want to fuck, nothing more?"

"Just two friends," she breathed heavily, rubbing me through my jeans.

"Now that that's settled," I said, reaching down, grabbing her ass, and lifting her to my hips. "Let's get started."

Fifteen

Ramona

Preston's fingers slipped between my folds as my back arched and I leaned into his lips as they trailed kisses along my neck. I hadn't expected to end up in bed together, but there was not a single thing that I regretted about it either.

All it took was a few dirty words about what he wanted to do to me, and I was stripping off my clothes in record time. I was beyond hot and bothered by him—I was full-on wet and ready to do everything he said.

He insisted that we go slow and refused to take his clothes off right away, but I wasn't about to complain about it when his fingers worked my clit over the way they were. He had only been touching me for a few minutes, and I already felt like I was going to come.

When was the last time a man had given me an orgasm?

I bit down on my lip and tried to keep from orgasming because I didn't want him to think I was some loser who could come from a single touch. I was already embarrassed that he knew about the details of my past with Daniel; I didn't need him to think I was also an unsatisfactory lover.

My breathing quickened, and I dug my nails into the sheets, trying not to give in and allow myself to tumble over the edge and succumb.

"Stop fighting it," he whispered in my ear, pressing his thumb against my clit and rubbing it while his fingers thrust inside. "Let go and come."

"I can't," I lied, squirming beneath him.

"Yes, you can. I can feel your body, Ramona. I know it's there. Give it to me. Now."

He lowered his mouth and pulled a nipple between his lips, sucking so hard that I yelped and arched my back. The change in position forced more friction against my clit, and I couldn't hold it any longer.

My hips bucked against his hand as I spiraled out of control, waves of pleasure washing over me as I pulsated against his fingers.

"Fuck. Fuck. FUCK!"

I panted, trying to catch my breath as I came down from the most incredible, mind-blowing orgasm I ever had.

"There, that's more like it," he said, lifting himself onto his elbow to look at me. "If we're going to do this, you can't hold back on me. I will make you come as many times as I want, Ramona. Come hell or high water—you're going to give them to me."

"It's not always that easy," I muttered, still trying to catch my breath. "I think you just got lucky with that one. I don't usually come easy. Well, technically, I don't usually come at all."

"What do you mean?" His brows pulled together.

"I can't remember the last time someone gave me an orgasm. Usually, my trusty rose gets the job done, and even then, it's starting to fail."

He rolled onto his back and scrubbed a hand down the scruff dotting his jaw.

"Please tell me you're kidding."

"About which part?" I started to pull the sheets up to cover my naked body, but he quickly reached over and stopped me.

"I don't think so. I'm not done admiring your body, nor am I done exploring it."

My cheeks burned as the heat rushed through them.

He rolled onto his side and studied my face as he chewed his lower lip.

"My favorite part was how wet you were for me, Ramona. I had no trouble sliding my fingers inside of your pussy. It was so warm and tight, ready to be fucked."

My breathing grew shallow as the ache between my thighs started again. I shifted positions, trying to make it go away.

"You're so fucking beautiful when you're turned on. I love the way you blush when I tell you all the dirty things I want to do to you. And I was right; you are a fucking firecracker, lighting up in the most glorious way as you come."

"It would be better if there were a lot less talking and a lot more action," I said, trying to steady myself enough to get the words out without letting him know just how desperate I was for him to fuck me right now.

"Is that so?"

His lips turned up into the sexiest smirk I'd ever seen.

"I'm starting to wonder if you're even as skilled and talented between the sheets as you pretend to be..."

He climbed off the bed and stood beside it, locking eyes with me and refusing to look away as he slowly undressed. He reached behind, pulling his shirt over his head before tossing it to the floor. I licked my lips, admiring the perfectly sculpted abs that I imagined were there all along.

I wanted to climb over, run my tongue along the ridges, and follow the trail of hair that dipped into the low-hung jeans that he was now taking off. He stood before me wearing nothing but a pair of snug-fitting black boxer briefs that were desperately trying to contain the erection trapped inside.

I looked back up at him, seeing the same desire on his face that I knew was on mine. He was holding a condom between his fingers, but I had been so distracted by his body that I never saw him grab it from his jeans.

He lifted it to his mouth and held it between his teeth while hooking his thumbs into the waistband of his briefs and pulling them down his muscular thighs.

Fuck. Me.

His cock sprung free, jutting up to his stomach as he opened the foil package and sheathed himself.

"You ready for me to prove myself to you?" he asked, his voice deeper than usual.

I was sitting on my knees at the edge of the bed, waiting impatiently for him to fuck me and put me out of my misery.

I nodded, smiling when he stroked himself while I watched.

"How do you want me?" I asked, licking my lips.

"That depends. What kind of orgasm do you want?"

I frowned.

"You mean there's more than one?"

He chuckled and ran a hand along his jaw.

"Lie on your back, legs lifted, and ankles behind your head."

My jaw dropped as I stared at him in disbelief.

"You want me to do what?"

"You heard me. Now go. I'm waiting."

I climbed back on wobbly legs and laid down in the center of the bed. I wasn't sure I was flexible enough to get my ankles behind my head, but I did my best. I hadn't been to yoga in a few weeks, so my body was tighter than usual.

I felt completely on display and didn't miss how his eyes zeroed in on my pussy. Instinctively, I started lowering my legs so I could close them, but he climbed up on the bed and stopped me.

"I don't think so," he growled before dipping his head between my legs and licking.

I gasped and let them fall to the sides again as he mercilessly tortured my clit with his tongue, nearly bringing me to another orgasm. I panted heavily, running my fingers through his short hair that I desperately wanted to pull.

"You taste as good as I thought you would," he replied coolly as he pulled away, leaving me throbbing with need.

"You can keep eating if you're not full yet," I teased, though I desperately wanted him to make me come again. That would be a first, and I really wanted to be able to say that I was one of those girls who had several orgasms in one night.

"Trust me; you'll come again soon."

I was about to object and tell him I couldn't come during sex, but before I could say anything, he lined himself up at my entrance and pushed inside.

There was a slight sting as he stretched me, but it was quickly replaced with the most incredibly full feeling I'd ever felt. I shifted beneath him, forcing him deeper inside.

He rocked slowly, letting me get used to him before he pulled out and slammed into me again.

"Fuck!" I cried out, digging my nails into his back as I bit my lip.

The angle he was fucking me at allowed him to rub against my clit in the most perfect way, but there was this other bundle of nerves deeper inside that he was hitting that made me feel like I was going to pass out and see stars from it.

He pulled out and slammed into me a few more times until he finally gave in and started pounding into me. I closed my eyes and arched my back slightly to get the angle I needed so he could keep hitting this new spot. I had no idea what it was, but it felt fantastic.

"Breathe," he said softly, leaning in close to whisper it in my ear before nipping my earlobe. "You need to keep breathing, deep, full breaths."

"Okay," I panted, trying to do as he said.

I hadn't realized that my breathing was so shallow or that I was holding my breath as I waited for an orgasm to build until he mentioned it.

His dick pounded harder into me as his thumb rubbed my clit, sending me into sensory overload as I tried to remember to take deeper breaths.

"Your pussy is so tight. I love how she squeezes my cock and milks it, taking everything I give her. It's going to feel so good when you come around me, your walls spasming so fucking hard as I pull every ounce of your orgasm out of you."

I whimpered, his words my kryptonite.

I'd never come during sex before and didn't expect it to happen so quickly. Before I could stop it, I was crashing over the edge, spasming around him just like he said I would. He continued to rub my clit with his thumb while his cock put pressure exactly where I needed it.

"Fuck! Fuck! FUUUCCCKKK!"

I closed my eyes and allowed my orgasm to consume me.

Sixteen

Preston

The lights had come back on during Ramona's climax, but it wasn't anything either of us stopped to notice. I couldn't get over how beautiful she looked as she came, and I tried desperately to push the thoughts out of my head about how I could watch that forever. The truth was that this was a simple friends-with-benefits arrangement, and nothing further was going to come out of it. Ramona agreed that she didn't want a relationship, and I wasn't willing to dive into the reasons why I couldn't be in one, even if I wanted to.

Her hair was fanned out across the bed, her lips red and swollen from biting them as she tried to fight letting go. I could tell she was close, and I wanted her to give in and let go sooner, but I also didn't know why she was holding back. Again, this was simply a friendly sex exchange, so I didn't need to get caught up in the emotional details. I was there to give her mind-blowing orgasms, and that was it.

I climbed off the bed and went to the bathroom to dispose of the condom, carefully holding the base of it to keep it from leaking out with how full it was. I knew that sex with Ramona would be different, but I hadn't expected her to be so fucking tight. Her pussy wrapped around my cock like they were made for each other, and drew out every last drop of cum when I finally exploded inside of her.

When I got back to the bedroom, she was wrapped in a sheet, looking into Louie's tank as she turned on the heat lamp for him.

"Everything okay?" I asked, standing beside her and not bothering to cover myself or my still semi-hard cock.

She glanced down and arched an eyebrow.

"I should be asking you that."

"I can usually go a few rounds before it goes down completely." I shrugged.

"A few rounds?" she questioned in disbelief.

"Mmm hmm."

"Oh my."

She pulled her lower lip between her teeth and clutched the sheet tighter to her chest.

"I was going to take a hot shower. Want to join me?" I offered.

"Ummm...."

I tilted my head and studied her.

"I've literally had my head between your thighs. Tasted your pussy. Felt your body as you came on my cock and fingers. There's nothing to be shy about," I said softly.

"I know, but that was before when the power was still off, and you couldn't see me."

I arched a brow but refused to admit to her that I had seen everything or that the lights had come on while we were having sex.

As if reading my mind, her face turned scarlet red. She reached up to cover it, forgetting about the sheet she was still holding against her body. It started to fall, but before she could recover it, I snatched it away and tossed it to the floor away from her.

"Preston!"

"I already told you, Ramona. You don't get to keep this away from me."

I pulled her into me and held her against my chest as her breathing evened out.

"Now, let's go get cleaned up so I can make you all dirty again later."

She giggled and let me lead her down the hall.

It only took a few minutes for the water to heat up, and then we were both standing inside, trying to keep our hands off each other. Just seeing Ramona naked and wet sent signals straight to my cock and made it hard again.

She immediately noticed and gave me a devious smile before lathering her hands with soap and dropping to her knees. I stood there with the water beating down on my back while she caressed my shaft and balls, cleaning me in a way that was addicting.

I leaned back slightly, allowing the water to run down my chest and wash the soap off for her. She grinned, and then once it was clean, she leaned forward and pulled me into her mouth.

I braced a hand against the tiled wall, trying to keep myself steady as my other hand wrapped tightly in her hair, pushing her head down further onto my cock. She opened her mouth further, taking me as far down her throat as possible while she worked the rest of my shaft with her fist.

"Fuck, Ramona," I moaned. "I'm gonna come."

She sucked harder, gripping the base tighter as she hollowed out her cheeks and continued. I could feel myself wavering on the edge as I tried to hold off. It felt so fucking good that I didn't want it to stop.

"I don't want to come down your throat," I panted. "Step back and let me come on your chest. I want to see my cum all over those gorgeous tits."

She gave me one last hard suck and then slowly pulled off, her mouth making a popping noise once the suction was broken. Then, without having to be asked, she leaned back and rested on her heels, pushing her breasts together as I jacked myself off and shot ropes of cum all over them.

It was the perfect image, and I wanted to lock it away in my memory forever. Once I was done, I extended my hand and helped her up. She locked eyes with me while she rubbed it all over herself, smearing my cum on her body.

Seventeen

Ramona

After we showered, I helped Preston check on the dogs and was pleasantly surprised to see Daisy and Rosco up and playing. He had found a ball and was rolling it around, bouncing around as he waited for her to try to take it from him. We refilled their food and gave them fresh water, then let them be since they were having fun and we needed to eat. We had already fucked three times, and my energy was dwindling.

While I thought it would be awkward to let myself hook up with Preston, I was pleasantly surprised that it hadn't been at all. He wasn't lying when he said he knew what he was doing in the bedroom and my body was still recovering from his touch. He'd made me come so many times in such a short period that I wasn't sure what I was going to do once this ended.

The power had stayed on for a few hours, so I was hopeful that it wouldn't go out again. I knew it would be days—if not weeks—before they cleared the roads out here, but as long as we had power, we were fine. While I had planned for supplies for myself for a few weeks, I hadn't accounted for having Preston there. But for now, we didn't have to worry about any of that.

"What do you want for lunch?" I asked, standing in front of a cabinet, going through the options.

He slid up behind me and wrapped his arms around my waist while planting kisses behind my ear and along my neck. He knew this was my weak spot and had fully been taking advantage ever since.

"You."

"I'm not lunch," I giggled, though I wouldn't necessarily be opposed to him eating me out again.

"Wanna bet? I've been craving a pussy sandwich."

"You just had one less than an hour ago."

"I know. I'm addicted and know what I want."

"You're crazy," I laughed, ignoring the wetness pooling in my panties again. "But unlike you, I actually need real food."

"Okay, how about this? We make you some lunch, and then I'll have mine while you eat yours?"

My eyes lit up as I spun around and looked into his. He was incredibly good-looking, and I couldn't get over how gorgeous he was when he was between my thighs.

"Fine," I sighed, pretending it was such a big inconvenience.

"Alright, let's make this quick," he said, smacking me on the ass. "I'm starving."

I laughed and made myself a quick peanut butter and jelly sandwich, thankful I had a new jar of jelly that hadn't been opened yet. As I was finishing up making it, he stood behind me and pulled the drawstring of my sweats, letting them fall and pool at my feet. I stepped out of them, trying to focus on grabbing the bag of chips I wanted while his fingers skimmed along my panty line.

I was already needy and aching for relief as I clenched my thighs together, trying to ignore it.

As if sensing my needs again, Preston spun me around, lifted me by the waist, and sat me on the counter. My sandwich and chips were right beside me as he nodded to them, made sure I had what I needed, and lowered himself between my thighs.

I closed my eyes and focused on the touch of his fingers as they feathered across my skin, leaving goosebumps in their wake. At that moment, I couldn't care about anything other than the glorious man between my legs.

I spread them further, inviting him in as I felt him chuckle against my thigh. I was totally lost in the moment when my cell phone rang on the counter beside me.

Now that we had power and I was able to charge my battery, I knew that I needed to take the call. That was the thing with living in a small town and being stranded in the middle of nowhere—if someone called to check on you, you better answer it.

I looked down at the caller ID and saw Maggie's name.

"It's my best friend, Maggie. I need to take this," I said, letting him know that he would have to wait a few minutes.

"Go for it."

He licked his lips and leaned forward, running his tongue along my slit through the lace fabric of my panties.

"Preston! I can't answer her call while you're doing *that*."

"Why not?"

"Because! It's…"

I couldn't think about what the word was that I was looking for because my brain was turning to mush as he plunged his tongue in deeper, the pull of the fabric brushing against my clit.

"It's hot as fuck?" he offered, pulling back slightly to look at me.

It stopped ringing as I missed the call, but I knew she would call back in a few seconds and keep going until she got me on the phone.

"What if she knows what you're doing?" I whispered loudly as my phone started ringing again.

"She won't."

"How do you know?"

"I don't." He shrugged. "I guess you'll just have to do your best to stay quiet so she doesn't hear you."

"You can't be serious."

My heart was racing, my palms starting to sweat.

His eyes landed on mine again and held my gaze as he slipped a finger under my panties and slipped it inside.

"You're so fucking wet right now, Ramona. You know you want to come. I want to give it to you. So, you can decide whether to tell her what you're really doing, but either way, I'm eating my lunch."

The call ended again, and I could only imagine how panicked Maggie was getting with me not answering. If I had power, that meant that her power had just come back on as well, so she knew that I should be able to answer my phone.

"She's not going to stop calling," he added, nodding to the phone in my hand as it started ringing again. "Better to just deal with it now. You handle that, and I'll handle this."

I lifted the phone to my ear and pressed the button to answer it.

"Hey," I said. My voice sounded strange, and I knew she would immediately pick up on it.

"Hey. What's going on? You sound different."

"Nothing," I lied. "What's up with you?"

I was trying to focus on what she was saying, but Preston's tongue darting in and out of my folds made it nearly impossible.

"You're lying. Are you being weird because you did

something to Preston? Don't admit it over the phone—I can't lie in court if I'm called in!"

I leaned back, closed my eyes, and ran my fingers through his hair as he sucked my clit.

"No."

"No?"

"What's she saying?"

I slightly recognized the other voice but wasn't paying enough attention to notice that I had been put on speaker phone. A soft moan escaped my lips, forcing Preston's head out from between my thighs as he gave me a warning look and pressed his finger to his lips to shoosh me.

"She hasn't said much. She's acting weird like she's drunk or something," Maggie answered.

"I haven't heard her say she loves you, so I don't think she's drunk," Dylan said.

"I'm not drunk," I muttered, still not focused. "I'm fine."

As soon as I said that, Preston pressed his face in closer and sucked my clit while his fingers curled inside and rubbed the spot that had been driving me nuts all afternoon. I wasn't fine—not at all. I was about to have one of the most intense orgasms while on the phone with my two best friends.

"You don't sound fine," Maggie noted, still unconvinced. "I know you didn't want to have Preston there, but I don't get what's happening or why you're being so strange. Is he like a serial killer, and he's now holding you there against your will?"

"No. I'm fine. Good. Soooo good," I panted. My legs trembled as I tried to keep them open while Preston continued his torture. "So fucking goooood."

Just then, Preston nipped my clit, sending a jolt right through me.

"Ahhh!" I cried out.

"You have to be quiet, or I'm not going to let you come," he warned quietly.

"What was that?" Maggie asked, suddenly more concerned.

"Nothing, I just stubbed my toe."

"Oh. That sucks."

I was thankful that Maggie bought my bullshit excuse and didn't press any further.

"I don't know, that didn't sound like she stubbed her toe," Dylan commented. "Before that, she sounded like she was—"

"What?!" Maggie asked.

I wanted to jump in and object, but Preston had increased his pressure as he brought me painstakingly closer to the edge.

"I'm fine," I panted, trying to say something so Dylan would drop it and move on, but I knew they could hear it in my voice. "Really fine. On top of the world."

"Ramona—please tell me you're not doing what I think you're doing," Dylan groaned.

"What do you think she's doing?"

Just then, Preston sucked harder, sending me over the edge. I bit down on my hand and pushed the phone away from my ear to try to keep them from hearing as I hissed instead of moaning.

I spasmed around his fingers, letting them take every last bit of my orgasm from my spent body.

My chest rose and fell heavily as I tried to catch my breath.

The other end of the line had gone so quiet that I wasn't sure if Maggie was still there. Preston stood up and wiped his mouth with the back of his hand, but it did nothing to remove the smirk he was wearing.

He helped me down and then left the room to give me privacy as I sat at the table and pressed the phone to my ear again.

"Are you still there?" I asked nervously.

"Oh yeah, I'm still here. And you're going to tell me everything," Maggie said, a hint of satisfaction in her tone.

"I don't know what you're talking about."

"Bullshit. Let's start with how you just let Preston get you off while you were on the phone with me and Dylan."

I covered my hand with my face.

"Did he hear everything?"

"No, he left the room once he guessed what was happening."

"Ugh," I groaned. "I'm never going to be able to look him in the eye again."

"It's okay. I think he's going to avoid you for a while anyway." She laughed, and I felt the corners of my lips turn up.

"It wasn't my fault," I said lightly.

"Yeah, I just hate it when an attractive man pins me down and forces me to come while I'm on the phone with my best friend."

"It really wasn't," I laughed. "I told him we couldn't do that while I was on the phone."

"And what did he say?"

"He said that I had to be quiet, or he wouldn't let me come."

"That's so fucking hot," Maggie squealed.

"I know!" I whispered, hoping he wasn't close by and hearing our conversation. "I didn't expect it either."

"We have so much catching up to do as soon as they clear the roads and get you out of there."

"Yeah, we do."

"Until then, I'll let you go so you can get back to wherever that was going. But now that I know that you're safe and alive, I won't call again until you tell me to. Let me know if you need anything, though it sounds like Preston is right on top of filling those needs," she joked.

"I'll call you later," I said, eager to find him and finish what he just started.

"Make good choices. But in case you don't, I just want to say that Maggie would be an adorable name for a little girl."

"That's not happening," I lied.

"Like hell it isn't. I'm just saying you guys are going to run out of condoms before the roads are clear, so make sure you're making smart choices unless you want to make me an aunt. I won't object to that."

I said goodbye and promised to call her later, but I couldn't stop worrying about what would happen if we ran out. The problem was that it wasn't really a matter of *if* but *when*.

Eighteen

Preston

I tried to busy myself with fixing Ramona's computer to keep from allowing the thoughts to intrude my mind the way they wanted to. The goal was to keep things between us limited as friends with benefits—simple fuck buddies—and not let the emotional side creep in. Emotions were the one thing that I couldn't handle and had kept locked away ever since the day my world had come crashing down around me. It tried to break me then, and I wouldn't risk allowing that pain to take me now. But the only way to avoid it was to not let Ramona close enough to risk it, to begin with.

She was messing around in the store, moving boxes of inventory that we hadn't gotten to before we had sex. Daisy and Rosco were running around, chasing her down every aisle and waiting for her to give in and give them another treat. So much for trying to keep Rosco on a strict diet like I had imagined. He'd consumed his weight in treats as we worked with him on obedience training. But as long as he was trainable and learned, that was all that mattered.

I was waiting for an update to finish loading when my phone rang. I glanced down and saw my mom's name on the caller ID.

"Hey, Mom."

"Hello. Just checking in now that the power is on. How are you and Rosco?"

"We're fine. How are you and Dad?"

"Good. We're used to these. Do you need anything? They're working on the roads, so we can probably get over there tomorrow since it's already getting late today. Don't want to chance driving on black ice once it all freezes over again tonight."

"No, thank you. I'm not at home."

"Where are you?"

I clicked my tongue against the roof of my mouth, not wanting to tell her that I had been stranded with Ramona because I knew she would automatically think there was something going on between us. Now that there was, I couldn't technically lie to her about it, but we definitely had different definitions of what this thing between Ramona and me was.

"I'm actually staying with a friend," I said breezily, hoping she didn't press any further.

"A friend? Who?"

"You don't know them." I looked around, trying to find Ramona.

"Preston Elijah Roberts," she warned. "You know damn well that you don't have any friends that I don't know about. Why don't you want to tell me where you're at?"

I sighed heavily, leaning back in the chair behind the counter, still unable to spot where Ramona had wandered off to in the store.

"I'm with Ramona Watkins."

There was a heavy pause on the other end of the line before an audible gasp escaped her lips.

"It's not what you think, Mom. I came by Cool Cats to get some supplies for Rosco—you know, the dog that was forced upon me at last minute? Anyway, I thought I could make it and get back before the storm hit, but I didn't."

"Is Rosco at your house by himself?"

"No, I brought him to the store with me because I didn't want to come home to him eating half of it while I was gone. He's made a friend with Ramona's dog, Daisy."

"It sounds like love is in the air over there," she said softly, something in her tone getting under my skin and making me squirm.

"Absolutely not," I bit out. "And it would be great if you pushed that thought out of your head before you start getting any other ideas."

"I was talking about Rosco and Daisy." She laughed. "But I am curious why you're so quick to react that way when you thought I was talking about you and Ramona. Did something happen there as well?"

"I don't have time for this, Mom. I'm glad you and Dad are safe. I'll check in once I'm home, but it'll probably be a few days before they get the roads out here cleared."

"More like a week or two."

My brows pinched together as I read the error message on the screen. That was not what I was expecting. I moved the mouse, clicked a few boxes, and opened a new window.

"Are you still there?" she asked, pulling my attention back to her.

"Yeah, sorry. I was working on Ramona's computer for her."

"That's nice of you," she practically sang, the joy in her voice unmistakable.

"It's nothing. We're stranded here, and I have time to look at it for her. Nothing more than that."

"Okay, honey. If you say so."

"That's exactly what I'm saying."

I could feel my blood pressure rising. My mom always knew the buttons to push to get under my skin.

"I didn't mean anything bad by it. I simply meant that it was nice that you were helping her. I'm sure she appreciates it. She's such a nice girl. It wouldn't hurt to get to know—"

"Don't," I warned.

"Okay, fine. I'll let you go but call if you need anything."

"Will do."

"Love you."

"Love you too, Mom."

I hung up and set my phone on the counter next to the computer. I closed my eyes and tried to force down the feelings that were bubbling to the surface, too raw to deal with right now.

"Hey, are you okay?" Ramona asked, coming around the corner with both dogs following behind her.

"Yeah, I'm fine." I cleared my throat and pulled her computer closer to me, using it as a shield. "Just running another update, and hopefully, I can get this fixed for you."

"Thank you. I appreciate it. I was going to go look at options for dinner. Anything in the canned food category that sounds good to you?"

"I'm good with whatever," I answered, refusing to look at her.

I could feel her eyes on me but kept my focus on the screen so I didn't have to see the hurt look on her face. It had only been a few days, and she had already managed to get to me, which wasn't something that I could afford to have happen right now.

Nineteen

Ramona

Preston had been acting weird ever since he talked to his mom a few days ago. I didn't bother to ask him about it because he continuously made it clear that our arrangement included physically pleasuring each other and nothing beyond that. But from what I had overheard of his conversation with her, it didn't sound too bad, just that he was stranded here with me until the roads were cleared.

While I could assume that his mom was hinting at something happening between us, I couldn't figure out why Preston had such a cold reaction to it. I mean, we were literally fucking like bunnies, so *something* was going on. But there was an uneasiness in his tone when he spoke to her, and the way his shoulders knotted with tension once he hung up that made me think there was something else going on.

Since we hadn't talked about it, my brain had jumped down several rabbit holes, wondering if Preston was truly bothered to be stuck there with me. It was probably my own insecurities that stemmed from my relationship with Daniel that had me feeling like I wasn't worthy of Preston's attention. Not only that, but since Preston made it abundantly clear that this was a no strings attached hookup, I felt myself wondering if it would even happen if we weren't stranded together.

I couldn't help but question whether the chemistry was really there between us or if I had been imagining it. The way he could be so affectionate with me while we were having sex was so different from how he interacted with me when we weren't. It was like hot and cold, two very different extremes, and I hated it.

It had been almost a week since the storm first hit, and I had been focused on the news reports to see if they were going to work the roads out here any time soon. I was on edge today and found myself praying that they would get to us ASAP so Preston could leave and be on his way. Maybe then I could clear my head and sort out the confusion that was constantly fogging my brain these days.

I leaned forward and turned up the volume on the TV, listening to the news anchor go on about how they were being forced to take a break from clearing the roads because another storm was rolling in.

"Ugh," I groaned, flopping back in the chair and shaking my head.

"What's wrong?" Preston asked, walking in and looking from me to the TV.

"They're not going to get the roads cleared because there's another storm moving in. Guess we're stuck together even longer now. I'm sure you're happy about that."

His jaw tightened as he pulled his shoulders back.

"What's that supposed to mean?"

I could feel the tension in the air between us.

"Nothing." I shook my head and got up, walking past him to the sink.

He grabbed my hand and stopped me. I froze, refusing to look at him even though I could feel his eyes boring into me.

"What's that supposed to mean, Ramona?"

I rubbed my lips together, still unable to answer him. I didn't mean to say it, and now there was no way to backtrack and pretend that I hadn't.

"Talk to me. Tell me what's going on. If you don't want Rosco and me here anymore, I can figure out a way to get out of your hair."

"It's not that," I said softly. "I just know that *you're* anxious to get out of here. That's all."

"Why do you say that?"

"Because you've been acting different lately. Ever since you talked to your mom."

I lowered my voice, ashamed to admit that I had overheard their conversation—or at least one side of it.

He sucked in a deep breath and slowly let it out as he pulled me against his chest and wrapped his arms around me.

"I'm sorry. Sometimes my mom gets in my head, and it messes me up. I didn't mean to take it out on you."

"You don't have to apologize. It's not like we're in a relationship or anything. We're just friends who are fucking, right?"

There was a hint of uncertainty in my voice that I hated. I didn't want him to worry that I was hoping this would turn into more, but I also couldn't deny that I hadn't imagined the *what-ifs*.

"Is that what you still want?"

"I don't know," I whispered, pressing my cheek against his chest so he couldn't see me. "The sex is pretty great, so I don't necessarily want to stop that."

"But…"

And there it was. The elephant in the room that we both had been trying to avoid.

"But I can't lie and say that I don't feel like there could be something more than just sex between us. I like you, Preston, and I enjoy spending time with you, even if we're being forced into it."

His body stiffened against me, and I could tell he didn't feel the same way.

"I'm sorry, Ramona. I can't do more than just sex. I'm not a relationship guy. We talked about that before any of this ever started."

"I know. I just thought maybe you might change your mind if you felt the same—"

"I can't," he snapped, letting go of me and storming out of the kitchen.

<u>Twenty</u>

Preston

I tried to force the hurt look on Ramona's face out of my head as I struggled to find a way to burn off the excess energy that was coursing through me. Okay, so it wasn't energy—it was anxiety, and it was about to consume me if I didn't do something about it.

I knew that I owed it to her to talk about what happened earlier and why I couldn't be in a relationship, but no matter how hard I tried, I couldn't bring myself to do it. Instead, I'd been hiding in the play area with Rosco and Daisy, throwing a Frisbee so he could at least burn off some of his actual energy while Daisy cuddled beside me.

Things had gotten hard and out of place quicker than I had expected. But at the same time, I never expected to get stuck here with Ramona, nor did I anticipate that we would end up in bed together. If anything, I would have assumed I would have to spend my time stealthily dodging and avoiding her since all I had ever seen was her violent side.

To make matters even worse, there was another storm rolling in, and they hadn't even had a chance to clear the roads out here yet. I'd considered packing Rosco up, putting my truck in four-wheel drive, and taking my chances, but part of me worried about leaving Ramona alone by herself. Who knew how long it would take them to clear the roads after the next storm hit, and even worse, what if another one came along before they could? She would run out of supplies before she would have a chance to get more and end up in a bad spot.

That was the other thing that kept nagging at the back of my brain was that while I was here and essentially keeping her company for the most part, I was also utilizing said resources, and we were going to run out even faster at this rate. I felt like I was stuck in a tough position, no matter how I looked at it.

Or maybe I was just grumpy because I hated that I was feeling something for Ramona and knew that I shouldn't. It wasn't fair to her to lead her on and make her think I could give her something I couldn't.

After two hours had passed, Rosco gave up on me and passed out on the comfy bed next to Daisy, leaving me no excuse to continue to hang out in there. I could, but I might as well write the words *pussy* on my forehead because that was what I was acting like by continuing to avoid Ramona.

I gave them both a quick pat and then closed the door behind me as I left. I wasn't sure where Ramona was, but it wasn't like the place was that big that we could easily avoid each other unless I just hung out in the store, which felt weird. I took a deep breath and tried to calm my nerves before I faced her.

Just then, my phone started ringing. Saved by the bell. I glanced down and saw my brother's name on the screen.

"Hey, Kent," I answered.

"Mom got a fucking dog?"

I bit back a laugh and just shook my head.

"Yeah, only now *I* have a fucking dog. But I can't complain because he really is cute."

"I don't even know who you are," he teased. "Anyway, I was calling to check on you guys and see how things are going. I heard Whiskey Mountain got hit pretty hard."

"I'm actually stuck at a pet shop in Fallen Oaks. I came to get supplies for Rosco and didn't make it out before the storm blew in. By the time I was heading out, I couldn't even find my truck in the parking lot, it was that bad."

"Shit, that sucks." He whistled through his teeth. "But I'm sure the company isn't bad."

"Mom told you?" I groaned. I hated when she gossiped, especially when I was the one she was talking about.

"That and I know that the only pet shop in Fallen Oaks is Cool Cats, so I figured that's where you're at. Be careful, though. Ramona can be intense."

"Yeah, I've witnessed that a handful of times already. She threatened to rearrange some vital organs a time or two."

"Sounds like her." He laughed, and I realized how much I missed talking to him.

"How are things in Fallen Oaks? Did you guys get walloped too?"

"We got a couple of feet, but they've already cleared the main roads, so it's business as usual."

"That must be nice. I can't say that I missed this."

"Yeah, but we have something that Atlanta could never have."

"And what's that?" I asked, leaning against the wall.

"Family. We miss you, man."

I sucked in a breath and held it for a few beats before I let it out.

"I miss you guys too."

"You know you can always come back."

"I know. But it's like I told Mom, I'll never know what I'm capable of if I don't spread my wings and fly. There's a whole world out there full of possibilities. I don't want to be tied down and forced inside the constraints of small-town life where everyone knows your business whether you want them to or not."

"I know," he sighed. "I'm just saying, maybe it wouldn't be bad to plant some roots, meet someone, and then go exploring the world together."

"Now you sound just like Mom."

"Well, that's because she gets her wisdom from me."

"I'm gonna tell her you said that. She won't invite you the next time she makes meatloaf."

"Sure she will. I'll be her favorite child again because her other one will have abandoned her."

"I'm not abandoning anyone. I just don't want to be tied down and responsible for anyone else."

My neck tensed as I said the words, and I could tell by the silence on the other end of the line that he was trying to give me a moment.

"What happened with Shelby wasn't your fault."

"I don't have time for this," I muttered, ready to end the call.

"You never have time for it because you choose to live in a state of avoidance instead of choosing to talk about it and work through your grief."

"There's nothing to talk about!" I yelled, my voice echoing off the walls. "Shelby wanted more than I could give her. She made ultimatums and demands, and when I didn't give in to them, she took her own life! I can't be responsible for that again, Kent. I loved her, but it still wasn't enough. I couldn't save her, and that kills me every single day. *That's* why I choose not to be in relationships and refuse to commit. It's not that I don't *want* that kind of life for myself; it's that I don't deserve to have it, and I'm not willing to risk having this happen again."

"You guys were young. She was sick. It's not going to be the same. You won't know unless you let yourself try to—"

"I have to go. Talk to you later."

I didn't wait for him to reply before I hung up and shoved my phone into my pocket.

Twenty-One

Ramona

I was jamming out to Cardi B while painting my toenails on the bed when Preston walked into the bedroom, looking angry and upset. I dipped the brush into the bottle and then spread some of the mint green polish across my nail while I tried to give him some space as he paced back and forth in front of me.

"Is everything alright?" I finally asked, putting the brush back into the bottle and tightening it. I waved my hand across my toes, trying to get the polish to dry faster while I waited for his crazy eyes to focus on me.

"I need to go running," he blurted out.

"I don't think that's a good idea. The other storm is already moving in, and we're supposed to get 6-8 inches tonight. Plus, it's already dark outside, and you don't know the area."

He rubbed a hand along the back of his neck and let his head fall forward.

"What's wrong?"

"Nothing," he lied, shaking his head. "I'm used to being able to work out at home and burn off energy when needed. I feel like I'm going crazy, and there's no way to release this build-up."

I chewed my lower lip, nervous to even suggest what I was about to. We hadn't had sex in a few days, nor had we talked about his comment earlier about how he couldn't do the whole relationship thing. I had given him his space while I locked myself in the bathroom and cried for twenty minutes straight. It was what worked for me, but clearly, he needed something else. Something more physical.

"I know a way you can release some of the tension," I offered quietly.

He looked up and his eyes scanned over my body before reaching my face.

"I don't know if that's a good idea."

"Maybe. But it's also not a terrible one either." I shrugged as if it didn't matter to me either way, even though my center was already starting to get needy just looking at him and remembering all the delicious things he had done to my body before.

He stared at me a bit longer without saying anything, making me nervous.

"Look, I'm not proposing that we *make love*. I won't even ask to cuddle after we're done. I'm just saying you need a release, and I wouldn't complain about having an orgasm or two right now. It's a win-win."

"What about what you said earlier?" he prodded, folding his arms over his chest.

"I won't lie and say that I don't like you, but my world isn't going to end over you not returning the same feelings."

Something flashed quickly across his face as his jaw tightened.

"I'm just saying, I know how to do this with no strings attached. I'm not worried that if we have sex that I'm going to fall head over heels in love with you, Preston. Hell, at this point, I'm starting to reconsider and might threaten to stab you again. Who knows."

The corners of his lips started turning up.

I tilted my head to the side and studied him.

"Oh, is that your thing? Does my violent talk turn you on?"

"You have no fucking idea," he growled, crossing the room and tackling me on the bed.

I laughed as he tickled my sides, making me squirm until my legs fell open and he inserted himself in between.

"Nothing changes, this is still just sex between two friends," he said, pinching my chin between his fingers. "Got it?"

"Got it."

"Good. Now if you're a good girl, I'll make you squirt like you've been dying to."

Twenty-Two

Preston

I was guessing when I said that Ramona would be a squirter, but the way she clenched around my finger as I worked her g-spot told me I was right. I placed the palm of my hand down firmly on her lower stomach, creating as much pressure as possible as I used a come-hither motion with my fingers to bring her to climax.

Curse words spilled over her plump, beautiful lips as she tried to fight coming but couldn't. In just a short time, I already knew Ramona's body better than I knew my own and could tell that she was on the verge. I took my time and made sure I focused on where she needed me so I could finally give her the orgasm she had been craving.

"That was fucking amazing," she breathed, resting her arm over her head.

I wanted to say *you're fucking amazing* but bit back the compliment before it could be misinterpreted.

"Now that I've had mine let's get you yours."

She rolled over, reached across me, and grabbed the condom from the nightstand. Her breasts hung in my face, inviting me to pull a nipple into my mouth. I reached up and pulled her on top of me, devouring her as if I couldn't get enough. She giggled and then arched her back as I sucked harder, bordering on pushing her to her limit.

I took the condom from her fingers and continued sucking,

only stopping for a brief second to open it before resuming my torture on her again. I rushed to sheath myself before grabbing her hips and lowering her onto my throbbing cock.

We both gasped as I slid inside her, stilling momentarily as I allowed her to adjust to my size. I loved how tight she was and never got over how well she wrapped so snuggly around me, squeezing and milking every drop of cum out of me when I came.

"Do you want me to ride the frustration out of you, or do you want to take me from behind and work it out yourself?"

"Ride me for a few minutes, and then I'll take you from behind."

"Sounds good," she said softly, closing her eyes and letting her head fall back as she moved her hips in the perfect rhythm.

I wanted to be in the moment and enjoy having sex with Ramona, but I couldn't. My conversation with Kent was playing over and over in my head, and all I could think about was Shelby and how I failed to see how much she was suffering.

I pinched my eyes closed and grabbed her hips, stopping her from moving.

"What's wrong?" she asked, concern heavy in her voice.

"Nothing. Let's change positions."

"Okay."

She climbed off me and waited beside me for me to tell her how I wanted her. The problem was that I didn't know. Nothing felt right. While I wanted to have her face down, ass up so I could pound my stress away, I couldn't stand the thought of using her like that. I wanted to look into her eyes and connect with her as we—fuck…

I slammed my hand down on the bed, startling her as she jumped back. I didn't bother to look at her before climbing down and heading to the bathroom to deal with my own shit.

My heart was pounding loudly as I stared at my reflection in the mirror, hating the man staring back at me.

How the fuck did I get to this point?

Up until now, I never had a problem having sex with someone and walking away from it without any emotions involved. But this was different, and I didn't understand it.

It had been four years since Shelby committed suicide and four years since I stopped believing I could have the kind of life I always wanted when I was younger. Her death rocked me in a way that I never saw coming and changed something so deep inside that I lost a huge piece of who I was.

What Shelby wanted from me wasn't that different than what any woman wants from a relationship. Love. Companionship. A best friend. A family. A house to call home. The only problem was that I had barely turned twenty-one and wasn't ready to settle down. I wanted to be wild and free, to explore the world before I was tied down with kids and a mortgage. I asked her to come along with me and go on these adventures together, but she said that wasn't the kind of life she wanted.

On our one-year anniversary, she gave me an ultimatum. Either propose to her and buy a house in the next six months, or she was going to walk away. I hated being forced into doing something I didn't feel in my heart, but I also didn't want to lose the first girl I had fallen in love with.

I gave in, and we looked at a few houses, but I should have known that Shelby would have already had one picked out. Everything had to be her way or nothing at all. We signed the papers, and she was happy until she wasn't.

One ultimatum led to another, and soon, she wasn't the same girl I had fallen in love with anymore. She was so obsessed with fitting in with small-town life and having what she thought she was supposed to that she didn't care about anything else. At one point, I wasn't sure that she even loved *me* anymore, but more so the idea of having the perfect husband/father for her dream life.

After a while, I started putting my foot down on her requests and decided that I couldn't go through with marrying someone I didn't know. When I sat down and broke off the engagement, she couldn't handle it. She threatened me with everything she could, but I ignored her and walked away. That was the last time I saw Shelby before she took her life in the house we were supposed to turn into our home.

Twenty-Three

Ramona

I sat in the bed, unsure of what to do. Sure, I had questioned whether I was good in bed after Daniel and I broke up, but I'd never had someone walk away during sex. This was a first, and it left me feeling rattled and insecure.

The clock on the wall ticked at an annoyingly slow pace while I waited for Preston to come back. After twenty minutes, I decided that I wasn't going to sit around and wait for him anymore, so I got up, got dressed, and made my way to the kitchen. I knew better than to eat through my emotions, but I also couldn't just punch him in the throat like I really wanted to.

It wasn't that I was afraid of him or feared the thought of being stuck here alone with him. It was that something had changed deep inside with how I felt about him, and it no longer felt right to want to punch him. And that pissed me off even more.

How dare he squirm his way through the deep layers I put up and work his way into my heart, only to turn around and try to break it.

I slapped some peanut butter onto a slice of bread and spread it aggressively with a butter knife before plunging it into the jelly and scooping some out.

"Why do I have a feeling that the peanut butter is me?" Preston teased from the doorway, casually leaning against the frame with his ankles crossed and arms folded over his chest.

I arched an eyebrow and glared at him from the side of my eye without giving him my full attention. I wasn't *technically* mad at him, but I was feeling vulnerable, and *that* made me angry. I set the knife down on the counter and put the sandwich together on a plate before grabbing the nearly empty bag of Cool Ranch Doritos from the cabinet.

We were going through supplies quicker than I had anticipated, but then again, I had only accounted for myself being stuck here and not having a whole other human to feed as well. The news said there would be a small break between storms, but they advised not going out if you didn't have to. Normally I wouldn't risk it, but running out of chips was literally a crisis that I couldn't afford right now.

"I know that you're mad at me, and you have every right to be," he said with a sigh, not bothering to move from his place. Probably because I was still standing close to the knife block and had a menacing look on my face as I angrily shoved the sandwich into my mouth and took a huge bite.

"I'm not mad," I bit out as I chewed. "I'm irritated. With you. And whatever the fuck that was in the bedroom a few minutes ago." I stopped and looked at my watch. "Or half an hour ago if we're keeping track."

He tipped his head back and exhaled heavily through his nose before pushing off the wall and heading toward me. I swallowed hard, trying to ignore how my body felt as he got closer and instead focused on the anger still billowing up inside. I needed it to keep fueling me right now because if I let my guard down even a little bit, I would fall even harder for him than I had already.

"I'm sorry that you're irritated. I don't blame you. And when you're ready, I'd like to explain what happened."

"Oh, I fucking know what happened," I growled. "Do you think you're the first guy who's walked away and not wanted to fuck me? Spoiler alert!! It happened all the time with Daniel. It's nothing new, I guess I just expected more from you since you *seemed* interested in the first place."

He closed the distance between us and took the sandwich from my hands before slapping it down on the counter beside us. My eyes widened with fury. He was lucky that it was just the sandwich and that he didn't mess with my chips. That would have been a war that he wasn't ready for.

"I didn't walk away because I didn't want to fuck you, Ramona. I would have loved nothing more than to be balls deep inside you, feeling that tight pussy grip my cock the way she loves to as I pounded it."

A bead of sweat dotted my brow as my temperature skyrocketed with his dirty words.

"I walked away because I couldn't stand the thought of using you for sex. Or treating you as if you were nothing to me just so I could get off and relieve some stress. That's why I walked away, Ramona. Because you deserve better than that."

"But I said it was okay," I objected, my mouth moving faster than my brain.

Don't sound so desperate, stupid.

"I know, but my head wasn't in the right place, and I couldn't bring myself to do it. Believe it or not, I've enjoyed spending time with you while we've been snowed in together. I've never once treated you as just some girl I'm fucking, even though that was the original plan—just friends with benefits. But I think we both know that this is more than that, even if we didn't plan for it to be."

He rubbed his thumb against my cheek as his body pressed harder against mine, pinning me against the counter.

"But I'm frustrated because no matter how much I want to feel those feelings with you, I can't. It's not something I can allow to happen, and I'm sorry for that. I don't want to hurt you by leading you on or making this into something more than it should be, but I also can't seem to keep myself from wanting to be around you. So, it's putting me in a complicated position where I don't know what to do. The only thing I do know is that I'm not willing to treat you like you're nothing more than a piece of ass to work my stress out with."

"When you put it like that, it makes it kinda hard to stay mad at you," I mumbled, chewing my lower lip.

"Well, I wouldn't blame you if you did. I acted like an asshole, and I'm sorry for that. I've had a lot weighing on my mind today, and I let it get the best of me."

I leaned into him and rested my head against his chest. His arms wrapped around me, holding me tightly.

"Can I ask you a question?" I mumbled, not wanting to lift my head to speak to him.

"Anything."

"What's the deal with you and commitment? I mean, I'm not asking you to be my boyfriend or anything, so don't freak out. I'm just curious why you're so against it."

His body stiffened beneath me, and I knew that he wasn't going to tell me.

"It's a long story," he finally said. "One that I don't want to get into right now. Why don't we go hang out and watch a movie or something?"

I decided not to keep pressing and gave in. We grabbed my sandwich, a handful of snacks, and some drinks, then crawled into bed to watch a romcom he picked, though I knew it was because he was trying to make me happy. For just a moment, I allowed myself to cuddle next to him and pretend as though we didn't have any cares in the world.

Twenty-Four

Preston

"Sit. Down. Stay." I did all of the same hand motions that Ramona did but Rosco looked at me like I was an idiot and refused to follow any of the commands.

"Why does he hate me?" I asked her, turning to see her working with Daisy on some light exercise. The dogs were going as stir-crazy as we were with not being able to go outside in almost two weeks.

Another big storm came on the heels of the first one, dropping another four feet of snow in the process. That wouldn't have been bad except that no one had been out on this stretch of road to clear it so we could get out. The temperatures rarely made it above freezing so nothing melted off either.

"He doesn't hate you." She laughed and stood beside me. "Sit."

She lifted her hand and made the same motion she had taught me, and sure enough, Rosco sat down for her.

"Good boy!"

I rolled my eyes and planted my hands on my hips as he took the treat from her fingers and wagged his tail excitedly.

"Okay, he's officially your dog now. He likes you better anyway," I joked.

"Well, he has spent a lot of time here recently, so I wouldn't be surprised if he thought this was his home."

"I'm going to have a hard time getting him situated when I finally go to mine, aren't I?"

She shrugged and tried not to laugh.

"I told my mom I didn't want a damn dog," I muttered. "He's going to eat my couch in retaliation because I took him away from Daisy."

"That I wouldn't doubt. They do seem to love each other." Ramona looked down at the dogs with a peaceful look on her face, like that of a mother seeing her child fall in love for the first time.

"Love is overrated."

My words slipped out before I could stop them, but thankfully, Ramona didn't say anything.

It had been six days since we'd discussed what happened in the bedroom. She hadn't tried to approach the topic of my fear of commitment since then, and I hadn't allowed anything physical to happen between us either. It was as if we'd drawn a line in the sand, and now both of us were scared to cross it. Instead, we just enjoyed our time together as friends, which seemed to be something neither of us minded.

"They really need some fresh air," Ramona said randomly, staring down at the pups who were looking back up at her. "I bet we could clear a path out front and let them out for a bit."

"Do you think the snow is blocking the door, though?"

"Only one way to find out." She grinned devilishly and winked.

I helped her get the pups leashed and followed her to the front door, refraining from laughing as she tried to force it open by throwing herself into it.

"Want me to try?" I offered, extending Rosco's leash to her.

"Be my guest."

It was already unlocked, but there was definitely a massive clump of snow blocking the door on the other side. I mimicked her, throwing my weight at it a few times until it finally budged. A gust of cold air whipped past us through the crack as I shoved myself into it until it finally opened enough so I could squeeze through. There was a shovel by the door, so I grabbed it and went out first, squeezing myself through the small opening and clearing the path for them to come out.

"It's freaking cold out here," Ramona complained, wrapping her arms tightly around her waist while gripping the leashes tightly. She'd recommended giving them a decent amount of leeway so they could stretch and explore without getting too far ahead of us and ending up in dangerous territory.

I offered to take Rosco from her, but she waved me off and said she had them. Since we were finally able to get outside, I took the time to clear a path from the door to the parking lot and cleared off the layers of snow from our cars. It was a lot of work, but the physical activity made it easy to ignore how blistering cold it was outside.

Ramona was walking the dogs in the path that I cleared, allowing them to stop and sniff the trees that lined the edge of the parking lot without getting too deep in snow since it would literally swallow Daisy whole. I cleared my truck and felt giddy and excited that I could finally see it again. Aside from the freezing temperatures, it seemed the worst of the storms had already hit, and I prayed that we wouldn't get any more snow so I could get back to my house and, even more important, back to reality.

I moved over to Ramona's car and started working on clearing the snow from around it. I was just about done making a path when she turned and scanned the area, trying to find me. I lifted my hand and waved, giving her a smile as I stepped to the side to brush the snow from the top of her car.

"Preston! Watch out!" she yelled, but it was too late.

I felt my ankle twist into an unnatural position as I rolled it and fell into a large pothole.

Twenty-Five

Ramona

"Keep the ice on it," I said, pushing the bag back over Preston's ankle.

"It hurts."

"I know. That's because it's swollen. It's like double the size of your other one. Now ice it."

"You're so bossy."

"You know it. Now stop arguing with me and do as I say."

I stood up and walked over to the shelf I had dedicated to medical stuff in my pantry. I leaned on my tiptoes, trying to find anything that could help. I had him resting in the kitchen with his foot propped up on a pillow on a chair across from him, but I knew that I needed to find something to wrap it with, or it was going to keep swelling.

He could walk on it—though not very well—so I didn't think it was broken. Definitely sprained, which was something I knew a thing or two about, given how clumsy Maggie was and all of the sprains I had helped her tend to throughout the years.

"I'm fine. You don't need to go through all this trouble," he said, shifting in his chair.

I turned to find him lifting the ice bag off his foot and scowling. He lowered his eyes and put it back, then looked away.

"I need to go to the store," I mumbled, closing the cabinet door and pulling my phone out of my pocket. Rosco and Daisy were hanging out with us in the kitchen, so I kept an eye out for them so I didn't trip as I typed out a text message to Maggie.

Me: Hey, do you remember what all we use when you sprain your ankle? I know you like soaking in an Epsom salt bath, but what else really helps? Tylenol? Ibuprofen? That wrap stuff?

I waited a few minutes for her to reply, knowing that her phone was likely already in her hands.

Maggie: What happened? How did you get hurt?

Me: It's not me. It's Preston.

Maggie: What kind of dirty sex moves were you guys doing that hurt him? Did he sprain his penis?

Me: No, Maggie. He didn't sprain his penis.

Me: We decided to take the dogs outside for some fresh air, and he stepped into a pothole while trying to clear the snow from my car.

Maggie: That's so nice of him!

Me: It is, but I need you to focus on the part I actually need help with. He twisted his ankle, and it's really swollen.

Maggie: Epsom salt

    Ibuprofen

    Reusable ice packs

    Flavored lube

    Compression wrap

Me: What is the flavored lube for?

Maggie: Because you're going to owe him one hell of a blow job for clearing all that snow for you and then another one to nurse him back to health.

Me: You're ridiculous. You know that, right?

Maggie: (shrugging emoji)

Maggie: Hey, while I have you, did you get the email that I sent?

Me: No, I haven't been online in a while. Preston is working on fixing my computer, and I didn't want to rush him. Apparently, it was really messed up, but he's almost done. Why?

Maggie: It's nothing that can't wait. But let's talk when you do read it, okay?

Me: Sounds good. I'm heading out to the store before the next storm moves in.

Maggie: Please be safe and let me know when you get there and back.

Me: I will.

I shoved my phone back into my pocket and then took the pups to the play area so they could rest and use the bathroom without bothering Preston while I was gone. I hadn't told him I was leaving yet, but it wasn't like he was in any position to stop me.

I made a pitstop in the bedroom and put on my heavy jacket, thick gloves, and snow boots, then ensured I had my phone, wallet, and keys in my pocket. I didn't need anything to slow me down and knew I had limited time to get there and back before it was too late. It was a gamble, but I was willing to go for it.

"Hey, I'm going to run out to the store real quick. Do you need anything while I'm there?" I asked as nonchalantly as possible.

His eyes whipped up, dark gray irises burning into me.

"You're not going out in that," he hissed, nodding to the TV where the local weatherman was pointing to a greenscreen illuminated with dark blue spots that indicated the storm that was rolling in.

"I don't have a choice, Preston. You need things for your ankle that I don't have here."

"My ankle is fine. There, problem solved."

I placed my hands on my hips and leveled him with a look.

"No, it's not. And we're almost out of other supplies that we need."

"Like what?"

"Umm, food. Toilet paper. Batteries. And you could do with an extra change or two of clothes so you don't have to keep lounging in my robe while you wait for your laundry to be done."

"Fine, I'm coming with you," he grunted, trying to push himself out of the chair.

I reached my hand out and stopped him.

"No, you're not. You need to rest. Keep your ankle elevated and ice it. I'll be back before you know it. If you think of anything else that you need, text me."

I didn't wait for him to answer before I turned and rushed out of the kitchen. I hated going out in this kind of weather, but right now, I didn't have a choice. I pulled my beanie down over my ears and lifted my scarf to cover my mouth as I pushed the door open and got whipped in the face with a frigid gust of wind.

I made sure the door closed behind me before I climbed into my car and headed into town, praying that the roads would be clear enough to get me there and back safely.

Twenty-Six

Preston

Ramona had been gone for an hour, and I anxiously waited for her to return so I knew she was safe. She had texted me when she got there and then again ten minutes later to ask me which brand of frozen pizza I preferred for dinner tonight.

I tried to keep myself calm and not freak out about her taking her sweet ass time at the store as if she had no worries in the world. Her computer was still sitting on the table where I had left it yesterday while it did some updates. Since I had nothing better to do and was trying to rest like she asked, I pulled it over and turned it on so I could fix it while she was out. It would be a nice surprise for her to come home and it be completely done.

I waited while it started up, smiling when her Vin Diesel wallpaper filled the screen. I cleaned up a lot on her computer and eliminated most of the programs that came up every time her computer started since she didn't need them. Once everything was finished loading, I opened a new browser window and was surprised when her email automatically opened on the screen.

I was about to click the button to minimize it when a message caught my attention.

From: askmags@spillthebeans.com

To: rwatkins@coolcats.com

Date: October 17, 2022, 5:47 am

Subject: Is this about you?

Hey! This email came into Spill The Beans, and every time I read it, it feels oddly familiar. I don't want to jump to assumptions but read it and let me know if you think so too. Love you!

Dear Ask Mags,

I've read your blog for years, and you've always been able to help other people, so I thought maybe you could help me too. You see, I've been madly in love with my best friend for over a year now and have never had the courage to tell her.

Before, I couldn't because she was with this guy who never treated her right. They started dating off and on in high school, and before I could shoot my shot, they moved in together.

They broke up a few months ago, and I was trying to give her time before I rushed in and told her how I felt, but now she's shacked up with someone else during the worst storms to date in Montana. I feel like every time I try to build the courage up to tell her, something gets in my way.

I want her to be happy, and part of me thinks that I'm the person who can do that for her if I could just get the chance. I know she's not meant to be with the guy she's stuck with right now because she could barely stand him before this happened. But I heard them doing stuff the other day, and now I can't get it out of my head that maybe she's just getting with him because she needs rebound sex to get over her ex.

Should I assume that's all this is and keep waiting for the right time to tell her that I'm in love with her? Or am I risking losing my best friend by crossing that line with her?

Heartbroken and lonely in Montana

I read the email a second time and hated that it did, in fact, sound a little familiar. Ramona had talked about her best friends— Maggie and Dylan, a handful of times, but I never got the vibe from her that she felt anything more than friendship for Dylan, unlike what he seemed to be feeling in this email if it was him.

I closed it out and told myself that I would pretend that I hadn't seen it. It wasn't any of my business, and I shouldn't have read it, to begin with. Just as I was about to close the email, another one popped up from the same sender. There was no stopping me this time as I clicked on it immediately and read it.

From: askmags@spillthebeans.com

To: rwatkins@coolcats.com

Date: October 21, 2022, 11:18 am

Subject: Holy Shit. This is about you.

Did you know that Dylan was in love with you?!?
It honestly never even crossed my mind, so I feel as
blindsided by this as I'm sure you're going to, unless
you already knew and never told me (you bitch!). Also,
I wonder if he's sending the messages through Spill The
Beans hoping you'll see them and know it's him. Maybe
this way, he doesn't have to risk facing rejection if he tells
you to your face. I don't know. What are you going to do?

Dear Ask Mags,

Do you know what's really unfair about the whole "friends with benefits" thing? When it's the wrong friend that they're having benefits with.

I'm so lost and don't know what to do. I've dated my share of women and have plenty of experience with relationships, but I've never been in the position of wanting someone who doesn't even know how I feel about them.

How do you cross that line and make them see you in a new light? Because I'll be honest, I feel like I'm invisible to her as anything other than a friend.

But the problem is that now that I know how I feel about her, I feel like her friendship isn't enough for me anymore. I want her love and companionship, and need to find a way to confess my true feelings to her.

She doesn't even know how amazing she is, and I want to be the one to show her. To tell her every day how much I love and adore her while helping her chase her dreams and build the life that she wants. I want to show her that with a little hard work and dedication, she can have the doggy daycare she's always wanted while being a successful, independent business owner.

I'm going out of my mind thinking about her being stuck in this storm with some guy who doesn't even know her, let alone deserves to have her attention. I need a way to get through to her, to show her with some grand gesture that I'm the man she needs. The one who will give her everything she could ever want and more.

More Than Friends In Montana

I exhaled heavily and pushed the computer away, regretting that I stooped so low and read her emails.

<u>Twenty-Seven</u>

Ramona

I had two carts stacked full of groceries and necessities
to get us through a few more weeks of being cooped up
together. Sure, Preston could technically leave and go home
since I was able to get out and get to a store, but I hated the
thought of him being at home by himself with a hurt ankle.
I knew that his parents had moved to Whiskey Mountain
a few years ago from our recent conversations; however, I
didn't know whether or not they lived close enough to go by
and help him if needed during the storm.

I had taken the liberty to grab some new clothes for Preston
and guessed his size since I wasn't willing to text him and
ask. He was already cranky enough that I was out at the
store, so I didn't want to make it worse before I got home.
I also stocked up on double the amount of Cool Ranch
Doritos I might need, just in case.

The store was busy with everyone stocking up again before
the next storm hit. It wasn't uncommon to get a lot of snow
in the winter, but the amount we were getting right now
definitely wasn't normal, and everyone was having a hard
time preparing for it.

After I paid, a few of the teens who worked there helped me
get it all loaded into my car, filling my trunk and most of the
back seat and floor space. Once I was situated, I sent a text
message to Maggie and one to Preston to let them know I
was headed back.

The snow had started falling, but thankfully it wasn't thick enough to blind me as I drove through it. I made sure to stick to a safe speed limit and gripped the steering wheel tighter as I headed straight into a thick cloud of white.

I tried my best not to panic and used my voice commands to make a hands-free phone call.

"Hey, where are you?" Preston answered, his tone strained.

"I'm about a few miles away from the store, heading back, but I'm stuck in a whiteout and can't see anything around me."

"Fuck," he muttered quietly, but I could still hear it.

"Okay, stay on the phone with me and go as slow as you can, okay?"

"Okay," I replied, my lower lip trembling.

It felt like I was stuck in this alternate universe, unable to see anything around me and having no idea if I was even still on the road or if I'd veered off.

"Can you see anything around you?"

"No," I whispered, trying to keep from crying.

"Hey, it's going to be okay."

I nodded though he couldn't see me.

"What did you buy at the store?" he asked, changing the subject.

I gripped the steering wheel tighter and tried to focus on what he was asking.

"What?"

"What did you get at the store besides frozen pizza and Cool Ranch Doritos?"

"How did you know I got more Doritos?"

My cheeks stung from the cold as they attempted to smile. I had turned the heater up to full blast before I left the store, and warm air was blowing directly at me, but it wasn't enough to counter the freezing temperature around me.

"Because I saw that you were almost out, and I know how crazy you get about them."

"I do not get crazy!" I laughed and it felt good. My shoulders relaxed a tiny bit, but I maintained my death grip on the steering wheel.

"Yes, you do. You threatened to cut me when I asked for one the other night."

"Because you tried to take the whole bag!"

"How else was I supposed to know which one I wanted?"

"There weren't that many to choose from," I objected.

"Because you had already devoured them and didn't think to save any for me."

"I told you from the start that they were off-limits and mine."

"It would have been nice if I had known the chip rule before I got stuck with you," he teased. "I could have made sure to have plenty of my own."

"Why? What kind of chips would you have stocked up on?"

"Funyuns."

"What?! Out of all the chips, that's what you're going with?"

"Hell yeah, they're the best."

I scrunched my nose.

"Nope. No way. They're too oniony."

"That's the best part."

"Well, I wouldn't have kissed you if you smelled like an onion all the time, so I guess it's a good thing you didn't have them."

My insides felt squishy as I processed my words and wondered if he was doing the same thing based on the silence on the other end.

"I do have a toothbrush, you know," he said, his tone more relaxed now as well.

"It wouldn't have been enough," I joked, relieved that some of the thick snow around me was thinning out, and I could see the faint outline of the road ahead of me again. "I can see the road again."

"Good, that's really good."

I heard him breathe out a sigh of relief.

"Do you see any mile markers? I want to keep track of where you're at."

"I can't see them. They're already covered in a few inches of snow."

"Okay, that's alright. We'll just have to go based on how long you've been driving then."

"Yeah, but I haven't been doing the speed limit. The store is about half an hour away from Cool Cats, but it took me forty-five minutes to get out here earlier before the storm rolled in. My guess is it might be an hour or two before I make it home with the speed I'm going."

"It's okay. We'll just keep talking. Just stay on the phone with me so I know you're okay."

"Now who's the bossy one?" I joked.

Suddenly my tires hit a patch of ice at the same time that a strong gust of wind came out of nowhere. Instinctively, I grabbed the wheel and gripped it harder as I removed my foot from the accelerator. I tapped the brakes gently and tried to steer in the opposite direction of where I was skidding, but another gust of wind gave me another push.

"Shit!" I exclaimed, panic fully settling in.

"What's wrong?"

"I hit a patch of ice, and the wind keeps pushing me off the road. I'm losing control!"

"Stay calm and focus, Ramona. Don't slam on the brakes and try to steer away from the skid."

"I am. It's not working!"

Another massive gust of wind caught the car at the right angle, sending it spinning off the side of the road and straight into a telephone pole. I heard a loud thud before my head whipped back, and the airbag exploded in my face.

Twenty-Eight

Preston

"Ramona! Ramona!" I screamed into the phone, my body going ice cold when she didn't reply. All I could hear was the sound of her horn blaring after the car hit something hard then the line went dead as the call disconnected.

I got up, ignoring the pain that shot up and radiated through my leg. I could walk on it so it wasn't broken, which was all that mattered right now. I rushed as quickly as I could into her bedroom, grabbed my keys and wallet, then pulled on my coat before running out the door and into my truck.

I worked on clearing the snow as quickly as I could. I didn't need much—just enough to see in front of me so I could get to her before it was too late. Thoughts of Shelby floated through my head, and I felt this instant stabbing pain in my heart when I thought about losing Ramona. Needing someone to get me out of my head, I grabbed my phone from my pocket, found my brother's name, and pressed send.

"Hey, what's up?" he answered on the third ring.

"Tell me that I'm not an unlucky bastard who loses everyone he loves."

"What's going on?"

"I need to know that I'm not some source of bad luck and that I don't kill everything that I love."

"You haven't killed me…"

I could almost see the stupid smug smile on his face.

"Well, that's not the best starting point. That would mean that I love your ugly face."

"Which you do. And you haven't killed Mom. Or Dad."

"Okay."

I wrapped my fingers around the steering wheel and focused on the road as the snow blew heavily across the highway in front of me.

"You still haven't answered me. What's going on?"

"Ramona went to the store to get supplies and I was on the phone with her while she was heading back. She hit a whiteout and couldn't see anything around her for a few miles, then it cleared up, but she hit a patch of ice and a gust of wind forced her car off the side of the road."

"Oh, shit. Is she okay?"

"I don't know. I'm headed to go find her now."

"Why would she go out in this weather to begin with?"

"I twisted my ankle earlier, and she went out for supplies. Plus, we were almost out of food and other necessities."

"How did you twist your ankle?"

"I was shoveling snow from the parking lot while she took the dogs for a walk. I didn't see a pothole and fell in it."

"Why didn't you just take her to your house instead of letting her go to the store? You guys would have been better off there since they will have the roads cleared within a few hours."

I swallowed hard, the bile rising in my throat.

"I don't take women to my house. You know that."

"So you would rather let her risk her life to go get stuff you need instead of sucking it up and allowing her into your space?"

"It sounded like an okay idea at the time. In all fairness, I told her not to go and tried to go with her when she insisted."

"And now?"

"Now I worry that I've killed another woman that I've allowed myself to fall in love with."

A single tear slid down my cheek, and I didn't bother to brush it away as the cold sting burned my cheek.

"You didn't kill Shelby. You know that. And you didn't kill Ramona."

"We don't even know if she's okay. I tried calling her back several times, but it went to voicemail."

"That doesn't mean that she's dead."

I released a shaky breath and pushed my foot down on the accelerator, more desperate to get to her than ever.

"Shelby was sick, Preston. You remember her mother telling you that. She had suffered from depression for years and refused to get help. It also wasn't the first time that she tried to commit suicide. You were not responsible for her death."

"Then why does it feel like I lose everyone I love?"

There was a heavy pause.

"Wait, did you just say that you love Ramona?" he questioned, ignoring mine.

"Yeah," I sighed heavily. "I think I do."

"You think, or you know?"

"I gotta go," I said, distracted by the sound of a car horn blaring in the distance.

Twenty-Nine

Ramona

My head throbbed as I tried to lean back and get the airbag out of my face. I tried swatting at it, but it wouldn't budge, and I didn't have the energy to keep trying. It was freezing, and my body was having a hard enough time staying warm.

I reached around for my phone but couldn't find it. It must have flown across the seat with the impact of hitting the telephone pole. The call with Preston had disconnected, and since I couldn't reach it to call for help, I knew that I would have to hope that he had heard the accident and would call for me.

I didn't know how much time had passed, but I was getting tired, my eyelids fluttering closed no matter how hard I tried to keep them open. It was exhausting but resting felt much better than fighting to stay awake.

I couldn't feel my feet or anything else for that matter, the freezing temperature numbing me from the inside out. Not having any other choice, I closed my eyes and allowed myself to rest.

I knew it must have been a dream when I was floating on a raft in a shimmery blue pool, the warmth from the sun beating down on my perfectly tanned skin. I lifted my tropical drink to my lips, pulling in a refreshingly cold sip that tasted delicious.

There was music floating around me, some pop song with a fun dance beat. I swayed my hips from side to side, moving with it until suddenly there was this deep base sound that didn't match the tempo. I frowned, irritated with whoever was interrupting my good vibes and dance party.

"RAMONA!"

I tried to open my eyes, but they were too heavy.

"RAMONA!"

I could hear sirens in the distance as the cold came over my body again. I pushed as hard as I could to wake up, but nothing happened.

Thirty

Ramona

"She'll need to stay overnight for monitoring," the doctor said to Preston and me as he stood beside me, squeezing my hand. "We'll let her rest, but if she needs anything, just push the call button, and we'll be right in."

"Thank you," he said, smiling politely at her, then turning to me after she left. "Hey, how are you feeling?"

"Like shit," I answered honestly, wincing as I tried to sit up more in the hospital bed. "How did you find me?"

"I heard the car horn and followed the sound. Then I called 911, and they were able to get to you and bring you to the hospital. You gave all of us one hell of a scare."

"I'm sorry," I whispered, my throat parched. "I didn't mean to."

"I know."

"You're supposed to be off your ankle and resting it," I scolded, pointing to it as I took the cup of ice chips from him.

He pulled a seat over and placed it as close to the side of the bed as possible.

"I don't care about my ankle, Ramona. I care about you."

"I know, but you shouldn't have been driving with it injured. You don't have the strength that you need to do things like brake or climb up into that big ol' truck of yours."

"I couldn't give a fuck about any of that. When I heard you get in that accident, my heart stopped. I couldn't breathe. I was so terrified of losing you that nothing else mattered at that moment. Come hell or high water, I was going to get to you and save you because there's no way in hell that I could stand to lose you."

A tear slid down my cheek as I heard the emotion behind his words.

"Do you know the reason why I said I couldn't be in a committed relationship?"

I shook my head, too terrified to answer because I didn't want him to stop talking. He was finally opening up to me.

"I was engaged to someone who I loved very much. But she wanted things that I couldn't give her. She started to rely on me for her happiness and blamed me for her unhappiness. One day, I had enough and called off our engagement."

He stopped for a moment and lowered his head between his hands, his shoulders tensing up.

"She committed suicide after that."

"Oh my God," I gasped, clutching my hand to my heart. "Preston, I'm so sorry!"

"Thank you," he whispered. "I don't like talking about it because I don't like to relive that part of my life. For so long, I've carried the guilt of her death with me and have allowed it to consume my thoughts of happiness. I've been so focused on keeping myself detached from everyone that I didn't know what to do when I started to feel something for you. It scared the shit out of me because I didn't want to lose you too."

"I'm not going anywhere, Preston. I promise."

"I almost lost you today, Ramona. And that scared the shit out of me. I've never fought harder for anything before in my life. Not knowing whether you were alive or dead was what motivated me to push through my pain and fear and to get to you. I couldn't save Shelby, but I would die trying if it meant I could save you."

"I'm so sorry that I put you through all of this. I should have just stayed home and figured out a way to make do until it was safe to go to the store."

"Don't be. I hate that you were in an accident, but I also feel that it put everything in perspective for me. Feeling like I could lose you pushed me to realize I wasn't afraid of falling in love anymore because I was already there. Now I was afraid of losing it all and had something to fight for. You woke up a part of me that's been dead inside for four years."

"I don't know what to say," I stammered, overwhelmed with emotion.

"You don't have to say anything. Just know that I love you, and I'll go to the ends of the earth to prove it to you. I know I might have some competition, but I'm willing to go after what I want."

My brows pulled together in confusion.

"What are you talking about? What competition?"

His phone started ringing in his pocket. He pulled it out and slid his finger across the screen to answer it.

"I need to take this real quick, but you might want to talk to Maggie and check your emails."

Thirty-One

Preston

"Are you sure you guys have time to do that? I know you have a lot going on with the B&B." I leaned against the wall while my brother confirmed a few details with his friend.

"Yeah, we can get out there in a few weeks once the roads are clear. It shouldn't take more than a day or two," Kent said.

"Perfect. Just email me the invoice, and I'll get it paid."

"Na, it's on the house."

"No, it's not. You can't just come do work for me for free. Besides, it's for Ramona, not me."

"Sure we can. Someone finally broke the spell and made my brother fall in love again. There's no price to put on that. I'll check in later."

"Alright, thanks, man."

I didn't bother to argue with him because Kent was riding an emotional high right now, and I wasn't going to be the one to bring him down.

I waited for the doctor to finish up with Ramona before I went back into the room. I smiled as we passed each other, pulled the chair beside her bed, and sat down.

"What did he say?"

"He thinks I can go home tomorrow at the earliest, possibly

Friday at the latest. They're waiting for a few more tests before he feels comfortable clearing me. Maggie said that Dylan is going over to Cool Cats to take care of the pups for us and lock up when he leaves."

"Did she say anything else about Dylan?" I asked nervously, not wanting to admit that I had read her emails, but I also wasn't going to start a new relationship built off of lies and mistrust.

She swallowed hard and folded her hands in her lap.

"She told me about the emails to Spill The Beans and read them to me over the phone."

I nodded and pressed my tongue to the roof of my mouth to keep from interrupting her as she continued.

"I'm guessing you saw the emails, and that's why you mentioned the whole *competition* thing earlier. But honestly, Preston, I had no idea that Dylan felt that way. It's never been on my radar, and he never indicated his feelings for me. It's totally one-sided, and I don't feel the same way about him. I love him as a friend, but that's it."

"Are you going to talk to him about it?"

"Yeah," she sighed sadly. "I need to. I just hope that it doesn't ruin our friendship."

"I think as long as you don't threaten him with any acts of violence, you'll be fine."

I winked playfully.

"Oh, don't worry. I save those for you," she teased, returning the wink.

I stepped out of the room to give her some privacy while she took another phone call from Maggie. Everyone was happy to hear that Ramona was okay and were either dropping by to see her or calling and blowing up her phone with text messages.

While she was busy, I took the time to reach out to the mayor to start discussing options regarding clearing the roads on that stretch of highway. This wasn't the first time that Ramona had been impacted by bad weather, but I wanted to make sure that it was the last. I also reached out to Maggie's boyfriend, Owen, who handled all the commercial realty in Whiskey Mountain, to talk about building in that area. If there were more businesses and housing options out there, maybe it would be given the same amount of attention as Whiskey Mountain when it came to road safety.

It felt good to get the ball rolling on stuff that would help Ramona, and I didn't bother to ignore the butterflies that were swarming in my stomach when I thought about having a future with Ramona.

Thirty-Two

Ramona
One Week Later

It took longer to get discharged from the hospital than I had wanted, but I was relieved that Dylan had stuck around Cool Cats to take care of the pets while I was away. I knew I still needed to sit down and talk with him, but I just wasn't ready yet.

Things had been chaotic ever since the accident, and I was still trying to get used to the fact that Preston had yet to leave my side. He'd been sleeping on a pull-out couch bed that looked anything but comfortable. I offered for him to sleep in the bed with me, but given that I had two broken ribs and a broken arm, he quickly declined.

By the time I got released and we made it to Cool Cats, Dylan had already left—no doubt avoiding me since I was with Preston. It was nice to be home and even more of a pleasant surprise that someone had arranged to have everything in my car delivered here before it was taken to a repair shop in Whiskey Mountain.

I walked around slowly, enjoying the feeling of being home as I made my way to the back to check on Daisy and Rosco. Preston led the way, making sure that he had hold of Rosco before I went in so he couldn't jump up on me. The pups were doing well, and I was thankful that Dylan had been able to come by and take care of everything.

We went to the bedroom, and I laughed at how Lily was spread across the bed as if she owned the place. She was the most independent cat I'd ever seen, and I could imagine she gave Dylan the cold shoulder while he was here since she never warmed up to anyone. I went over to check on Louie and smiled when I saw Lily climb down as soon as she saw Preston walk in. She leaned into him as she rubbed herself against his leg and purred.

Preston grinned before bending down to scoop her into his arms. I was surprised by their interaction, but then again, I shouldn't have been given how much time Preston had spent here recently. Aside from Daniel, Lily didn't really know anyone else, and even then, she never acted like she liked Daniel the way she was with Preston right now.

I dropped some food into Louie's tank and did a quick check to make sure he had everything he needed. The humidity level was perfect, and the UV light had been turned on so he didn't need anything from me at the moment.

I sat down on the bed and took a moment to catch my breath. I was still exhausted and couldn't wait to sleep in my own bed tonight.

"You doing okay?" Preston asked, standing in front of me and caressing my cheek with his thumb.

"Yeah, I'm just tired."

"You don't have to go today. You can wait a few days until you're feeling better."

"I think it's better to just go and get it over with. The sooner we talk about it, the sooner things will go back to normal."

"Are you sure?"

I nodded and let my shoulders fall with my exhale.

"Okay, well, I'm still driving you. I don't want you going on your own."

"You do know that someday I'll have to go back to being on my own again, right?"

He sat down beside me, the bed dipping with his weight.

"I know. But not yet. Not today. I'm not ready."

"Okay."

I leaned into him and let him hold me, his arms wrapping gently around me.

An hour later, I had showered and changed into clean clothes, which felt amazing. Preston helped me climb into his truck since I was still without a car. It turned out that it would cost more to fix the damage that was done in the accident than it would to just buy a new car. I filed the insurance claim and was waiting for them to process it while I shopped for the perfect vehicle.

We pulled up to La Salsa, and Preston quickly jumped out and rushed around to assist me. It was nice to be pampered, but I hated the pain that came with it. I still had some pain meds I could take if I needed them, but I wanted to be in a clear mindset when I talked to Dylan, so I decided to skip them.

I kissed Preston and sent him on his way while I went inside and looked for Dylan. I spotted him at the table in the corner where we always sat and made my way over.

"Hey," he said nervously, standing up and pulling at his freshly ironed button-down shirt.

"Hi." I reached up and pulled him in for a hug, making sure that he knew first and foremost that I didn't think any differently about him now that I knew how he felt about me. "Thanks for meeting me for lunch today."

"Thanks for the invite." He laughed tensely and then took the seat across from me as I sat down. "I hope you don't mind, but I already ordered for us. I thought it might help so you didn't have to stand in line. I got you a number 5, extra sour cream, extra guacamole, and a side of queso."

"That's perfect. I appreciate it."

"No problem." He rubbed his hands together and scanned the room, looking everywhere but at me.

I steadied myself and took a few deep breaths, hoping my energy would transfer to his and calm him down, but it didn't. I knew I promised Preston that I would save the physical acts of violence for him, but I couldn't deny that my fingers weren't itching to reach out and smack him around a time or two. Just to knock some sense into him.

"Okay, enough!" I blurted out, startling a lady at the table across from us. I smiled and gave her a slight wave before turning my attention to a red-faced Dylan. "I'm sorry, but you're driving me crazy with how anxious you are. You need to chill out and just relax."

"That's a lot easier said than done," he said tightly. "You didn't admit that you were in love with your best friend through some tequila-inspired emails to your other best friend's online dating advice blog."

"No, but I did threaten to stab a guy in the liquor aisle if he didn't pretend to be my boyfriend after running into my ex." I shrugged and watched the shock and humor roll across Dylan's face.

"You what?!"

I nodded and leaned back so the waiter could set our plates down.

"Yup. I was getting stuff before the first storm hit, and Daniel surprised me while I was shopping for wine. Preston ended up being there at the same time, so I threatened him and forced him to pretend to be my boyfriend."

"So, are things between you guys still pretend…" His voice trailed off as I saw the sadness creep over his face when I shook my head.

"No, that was only in the store while Daniel was there. We really did get stuck together at Cool Cats when the storm hit, and then things sort of just happened between us. There was this chemistry we couldn't fight, so we decided to give in and see what it was all about."

"Does he make you happy?"

"He does."

I didn't even hesitate to answer him because there was nothing I was more certain of than how much Preston made me happy.

"I'm sorry, Dylan. I had no idea how you felt."

"Don't be. It's my fault for not saying something sooner."

"How long have you known?" I asked cautiously, lifting a bite to my mouth while he thought about his answer.

"I don't know. I guess I've always been in love with you but never let myself think about it because you were with Daniel. Then when you guys broke up, I found myself feeling more protective over you, but it still didn't occur to me why. I think I finally figured it out when I *heard* you that night on the phone. Something snapped inside of me, and it wasn't that I didn't want to hear it because I was your friend, and it was inappropriate. I didn't want to hear it because I was furious that someone else was touching what should have been mine."

I kept eating, unsure of what to say to that. Thankfully, our waitress chose that moment to come check on us and see if we needed anything. She smiled at me before turning her attention to Dylan, shamelessly flirting with him as if I weren't sitting there. Once she left, I set my fork down and leaned in so only he could hear me.

"That girl was trying to take you back to her place! She didn't even care that I was sitting right here!"

"Eh, she's not my type."

I lowered my eyes and felt my shoulders fall. I looked

around, needing something to distract myself from feeling guilty about not feeling the same about him.

"You're going to meet the right girl, Dylan. I promise."

"I know."

He reached over and squeezed my hand gently before changing the conversation to a new blog post he had seen on Spill The Beans. I leaned back and covered my mouth as I tried to keep from spitting out my food as I laughed. This was what I loved about Dylan, and I was thankful that it was still there for us.

Thirty-Three

Preston

I was anxious the entire ride home after picking Ramona up from lunch with Dylan. It wasn't that I was worried about her having lunch with her best friend, who had confessed he was in love with her. It was that I had an entire crew at her house, working on bringing Cool Cat's Dreamland to life, and hadn't told her.

Kent had gotten there a few minutes after I dropped Ramona off earlier, and by the time I got there, there were five trucks with guys geared up and ready to go to work. While working on her computer a few weeks ago, I found a design she'd created for what she wanted the Dreamland to look like. I asked her about it, and her face lit up as she talked about the different sections she wanted but never had the time or money to get it started.

I sent the blueprint to Kent and asked him how much it would cost and whether it would be doable. While she was in the hospital, we spent time going over the small details, and he confirmed that his crew could come out this weekend to get it done. With a handful of guys on the job, they could complete it in a few days.

When I left to go pick Ramona up, they were erecting walls and pouring a foundation for the room addition that she had mentioned but wasn't part of the original plan. She had told me recently that the only thing she wished she had was a living room with a fireplace and large floor-to-ceiling windows. If she had those things, it would be the perfect house-slash-work combo.

So, I took the initiative to ask Kent about adding an additional room off the back of the building and turning it into the living room she wanted. They were only doing the physical part of it, the interior decoration would still be up to her.

When we pulled up, she frowned when she spotted the trucks and leaned forward to get a glimpse of the guys working in the back.

"What in the world is going on?" she asked, pulling back when it hurt.

"It's a surprise."

I put the truck in park and helped her down before walking her to the back and holding her steady so she didn't fall. The snow and ice had been cleared, but I still didn't trust anything when it came to her safety. I might have been a bit overprotective, but I wasn't willing to see her get hurt again.

"Ramona, this is my brother, Kent. Kent, this is Ramona." I smiled as they shook hands, a puzzled expression still playing on her face.

"It's a pleasure to meet you. I've heard a lot about you," Kent said with a wink in my direction.

"What is all of this?"

Kent stepped to the side and extended his arm.

"Welcome to Cool Cat's Dreamland."

"What?" Her eyes bulged as she whipped around to look at me. "You're kidding me, right?"

"Nope." I shook my head. "It's all being built from your blueprint, but if you want to change anything, just tell Kent, and he'll make sure it's taken care of."

Her eyes filled with tears as she looked between us.

"I can't afford this," she whispered, nervously tucking a strand of hair behind her ear.

"You don't have to worry about that," I assured her.

"We're taking care of it," Kent added. "As well as the room addition."

"Room addition?" She raised her eyebrows.

"Follow me."

I grabbed her hand and gently led her to the other side, stopping a safe distance from where the guys were working.

"They're able to add on at the back of the building. So where your bedroom currently ends, there will be a living room on the other side. There's also an extra bathroom being added in as well as I know that was on your dream board. We'll go over the layout, but like I said, if you want to change anything, just tell us. We'll make it happen."

The guys continued working on pouring the footing while she stared on in disbelief.

"I can't believe you did this for me," she whispered.

"For us," I corrected, pulling her into me.

"Oh really?" she cocked an eyebrow.

"Yeah, I was thinking you could keep sharing your bed with me."

"We're back to that again?" she teased, using the words I'd thrown at her the first time I stepped into Cool Cats on me now.

"You bet your ass. Now are you going to share it with me or not?" I pulled her gently against me and lightly tickled her sides.

"Alright, I guess I'll share my bed with you. But only because you're going to be in it with me tonight anyway."

She wiggled her eyebrows playfully as I leaned in and captured her lips with mine.

Epilogue

Ramona

Nine Months Later

"Okay, I think everything is ready," I said nervously, stepping back to look at the banner we'd hung in front of the entrance to Cool Cats Dreamland.

Maggie and Dylan were already inside, getting the rest of the decorations set up for the grand opening.

"It looks great," Preston said, wrapping his arms around my waist.

"I can't believe this is finally happening. It's been a dream for so long, it's crazy to think that it's actually reality. Thank you for everything you did to get this going."

I turned and wrapped my arms around his neck.

"It was nothing."

He planted a kiss on my forehead, making me melt beneath his touch. That and it was the middle of summer and already hot as heck outside.

"It was definitely more than nothing. It was weather-related delays with the construction. A random lumber shortage. There was an influx of new businesses around us utilizing the same resources we needed. It was a heck of a lot, and I appreciate everything you did to pull it together."

"Don't forget everything *I* did," Kent teased as he brushed past us, carrying a tray full of baked goods. "I made the magic happen."

"Maybe with getting the place built, but we all know that I make the real magic happen where it matters," Preston joked, pulling me closer so I could feel his cock. Thank God it wasn't hard right now—there would be no way to explain *that* level of excitement to everyone when we opened the doors.

"Don't be gross," his mom scolded, smacking him upside the back of his head. "Everything looks great, sweetie. We're so happy for you!"

She pushed Preston out of the way and pulled me in for a hug.

I'd gotten to know his family over the past nine months and simply adored them. It was nice having everyone so close, but I still couldn't get over them constantly thanking me for bringing Preston home.

Shortly after we started the construction to remodel Cool Cats, I asked him to move in with me. It was a bold move, but I had never been more sure of anything before in my life. He said yes without even an ounce of hesitation and got to work selling his house in Atlanta. We took a trip out there after Thanksgiving, packed everything up, and moved into my place.

We quickly realized that we needed a little more room for both of us to live comfortably and added an office for him along with the new living room and extra bathroom. I also took the time to restructure things in the store and created a new storage system for excess inventory which helped us maximize the existing space so we could focus on the home side of it.

"Everything is set up inside," Maggie said, joining us in the store. "We can open the doors whenever you're ready."

"You're not going to make everyone have a password to get in?" Dylan asked, his brows frowning.

"I am. I just posted it a few minutes ago."

"Oooh, what is it?" Maggie asked, clapping her hands.

I think she loved the daily passwords more than anyone.

I was about to tell them when Preston turned and interrupted me.

"About that," he said, clearing his throat. "I changed it."

"You changed it? To what?"

"Why don't you go online and see for yourself?"

I eyed him suspiciously as I pulled my phone out of my pocket and pulled up the webpage. Things worked so smoothly, and everything ran faster now that I had 24/7 tech support in-house. I was beyond grateful for Preston giving my online store the upgrade it needed and for making everything easy to find.

I clicked on the link for the password of the day and felt Preston move in front of me.

"Okay, today's password has been updated to *Ramona will you marry*—" I stopped and covered my mouth, finding Preston in front of me on one knee with a ring box in his hand.

There were whispers as everyone oohed and ahhed, but I couldn't focus on anything other than the incredible man kneeling before me.

"Ramona, I love you more than life itself. You've awakened a part of me that I thought I would never feel again and have brightened even my darkest days. I can't imagine living without you by my side, so will you please marry me?"

I nodded my head as tears pooled down my cheeks.

"Yes! Yes, I'll marry you!"

He stood up and placed the ring on my finger before lifting me in the air and twirling me in his arms.

I was on cloud nine, feeling on top of the world. We smiled and hugged everyone as they came around to congratulate us. I didn't want to rush the moment but knew that we needed to open the doors soon before there was a huge line outside.

Preston had rallied with everyone in Whiskey Mountain and Fallen Oaks to make today's grand opening as massive as possible. There was even going to be press coverage, with a few of the local news channels coming by to do interviews and live videos.

"I just updated the password back to what you originally had it as," Preston said, pulling me into him once we had a minute to ourselves. "Toodles Poodles is the password for today." He raised his voice, making sure everyone heard as they all scattered to help out where needed.

I took a deep breath and pulled my shoulders back, ready to take the next step in my career.

"Okay, open the doors," I announced, squeezing Preston's hand as nerves shot through me again.

I was overwhelmed by the number of people that I knew who had come in and brought their fur babies to check out Dreamland. Maggie was situated at the desk, signing people up for reservations while I circulated throughout the room, saying hi and introducing myself to the people I didn't know.

With all of the new businesses that had recently popped up, there were a lot of faces I didn't recognize. We had people coming from all over Montana, buying houses and setting up shops in the new *booming* part of town. I was thankful for the jump in business but couldn't believe the long line of people flooding Maggie's table, all wanting their chance to bring their pets to Dreamland.

I took a moment and walked over to the corner of the room where Dylan was standing, leaning against the wall.

"Hey," he said, smiling at me and pulling me in for a hug.

"Congratulations on the grand opening. It's incredible."

"Thank you, it really is. I can't believe it's actually happening."

I looked around the room in awe.

"And congratulations on the other thing, too," he said, clearing his throat.

"On my engagement?"

I softened my tone and turned to face him.

"Yeah, that. Congratulations on your engagement. Happy looks great on you."

"Thank you."

I slowly pulled a breath in and held it for a few seconds, trying to figure out what to say to him. Things hadn't been weird for us since we talked about everything right after he confessed he had feelings for me, so I wasn't sure whether this was him being jealous of me getting engaged to Preston because he still had feelings for me or if it was something else.

"You're going to find the right girl someday, Dylan. I just know she's out there waiting for you."

"Yeah, maybe."

I raised my eyebrows and pressed my lips together. I hated seeing him so down.

"She is. Be patient because it's going to happen for you."

"I doubt it," he said, shoving a hand through his hair. "All I seem to find is the *wrong* girl. I think I've pretty much made my way through the decent girls in Whiskey Mountain—the joys of living in a super small town." He laughed, but it was forced.

I turned and leaned against the wall next to him. There were even more people filling the space now, and soon, there wasn't going to be room for everyone to be in Dreamland.

"Hi! Sorry to interrupt you guys, but can you tell me where I can find Ramona Watkins?"

"That's me," I said, raising my hand and noticing the blush that flushed across the girl's pale cheeks.

"Oh, hi! Sorry, I'm new in town and haven't had a chance to meet many people yet. I own Cravings, the new restaurant across the street, and Preston had asked me to cater some of the appetizers for the grand opening."

"Yes! I'm sorry; there's been so much going on. I totally spaced your name."

"It's Calli."

She extended her hand to shake mine.

"It's nice to meet you, Calli. And thank you so much for helping out with the food."

"No problem. It's my pleasure. I just needed to see where you wanted me to set up."

I couldn't help but notice the way Calli and Dylan kept passing curious glances at each other, so I took it as a sign from the universe to help things along.

"I need to get in there and help sort out some scheduling conflicts," I lied, gently placing a hand on Dylan's shoulder and shoving him forward. "But my friend Dylan would be more than happy to help you get set up. There's space in the store, right across from the register. If you want to set up there, we'll make an announcement to let people know to come by and grab some food."

"Sounds perfect, thank you."

Calli smiled up at Dylan, tucking her curly blonde hair behind her ear as he guided her through the crowd of people and into the store.

"What was that all about?" Preston asked, joining me as I headed toward Maggie.

"Nothing," I said with a shrug. "Just helping someone else find their happily ever after now that I have mine."

****

Ready for more Whiskey Mountain? Grab Dylan's story here: https://books2read.com/u/3yVzgB

Don't forget to grab your free copy of Finding Love In Apartment 2C—it's a steamy novella about a romance author who goes to great extremes to find the inspiration she needs for those pesky love scenes.

https://BookHip.com/VSWBGAM

Other Books By Samantha Baca

<u>The Haven Brook Series</u>
<u>(small-town romantic suspense):</u>

'Til Death Do Us Part (Haven Brook Book 1)

https://books2read.com/u/m2RJNR

The Cradle Will Fall (Haven Brook Book 2)

https://books2read.com/u/b6O0QE

The Ties That Bind (Haven Brook Book 3)

https://books2read.com/u/mqgoz8

A Very Haven Christmas (Haven Brook Book 4- Novella)

https://books2read.com/u/mvqGjj

Three Strikes, You're Gone (Haven Brook Book 5)

https://books2read.com/u/mvqL2z

<u>The Dark Shadows Trilogy (romantic suspense)</u>

Five Steps Ahead (Dark Shadows Book 1)

https://books2read.com/u/38Q0gO

Ten Seconds Too Late (Dark Shadows Book 2)

https://books2read.com/u/3JRgVB

Against The Clock (Dark Shadows Book 3)

https://books2read.com/u/m2YwoR

The Stone Creek Series (small-town- novellas)

Chocolate Covered Mistletoe (Stone Creek Book 1)

https://books2read.com/u/3LRk9N

Candy Coated Promises (Stone Creek Book 2)

https://books2read.com/u/mldP5Y

Pumpkin Spiced Possibilities (Stone Creek Book 3)

https://books2read.com/u/bojdwV

Beaumont Creek Series (small town)

Just One Time (Beaumont Creek Book 1)

https://books2read.com/u/3G52zK

Second Chances (Beaumont Creek Book 2)

https://books2read.com/u/4Aj6Z0

Third Time's The Charm (Beaumont Creek Book 3)

https://books2read.com/u/b5lEyG

Four-ever Single (Beaumont Creek Book 4)

https://books2read.com/u/4j5jMX

Fifth Wheel (Beaumont Creek Book 5)

Preorder link coming soon

Whiskey Mountain Series (small-town- novellas)

Something To Talk About

https://books2read.com/u/4X62ag

Something To Think About

https://books2read.com/u/3GWAan

Something To Believe In

https://books2read.com/u/3yVzgB

Something To Live For

Preorder link coming soon

Sugarplum Falls Series
(Holiday Novellas- can be read as standalone)

Blame It On The Mistletoe

https://books2read.com/u/bw1rqe

Blame It On The Eggnog

https://books2read.com/u/38PPY6

Blame It On The Candy Canes (coming 11/3/23)

https://books2read.com/u/31DNo7

Blame It On The Blizzard (coming 11/17/23)

https://books2read.com/u/b6z6XE

<u>Standalone Books</u>

One Last Wish

https://books2read.com/u/mqg7D9

Finding Love In Apartment 2C (novella)

https://books2read.com/u/bze9aZ

Cocky Counsel: A Hero Club Novel

https://books2read.com/u/31Kzkn

All Is Fair In Food And War (novella)

https://books2read.com/u/bp8qjX

<u>Holiday Books (novellas)</u>

Snow Place To Go

https://books2read.com/u/4A560N

A Christmas Wish

https://books2read.com/u/4EKXpE

Holiday Hijinks

https://books2read.com/u/4DP6Ze

Acknowledgments

Thank you to everyone who has taken the time to read this book! It means the world to me, and I greatly appreciate your support!

Amanda, thank you for taking this one on and giving me so much feedback along the way. I really don't know what I would do without you! I know I would probably go crazy, so let's not try that out, okay? Okay.

To my beta readers, Claire, Jennifer, Natasha, and Malissa, thank you for reading this one early and for the excitement and enthusiasm over Preston and Ramona. I loved getting your messages, and your feedback was also so incredibly helpful!

Thank you to all of my ARC readers who grabbed a copy as soon as it was available—you guys are amazing, and I am so honored to have you on my ARC team!!

As always, I want to say thank you to my family for their constant love and support. Thank you to my friends for always being there for me and for shouting about my books from the top of the highest mountains.

A huge thank you to my amazing husband, who stands by me constantly and never stops pushing me to do better and go after my dreams. I love you, baby, and you're still the best book boyfriend I've ever had (wink, wink).

To my girls—never doubt your abilities when doing something challenging. Let this be proof that if you're truly determined, anything can happen.

About the Author

Samantha lives in the southwest with her husband and two small children after abandoning her childhood dream of living in a cabin in Colorado when she found that she couldn't afford to live there and was deathly allergic to the woods. When she's not writing, she's usually spouting off sarcastic remarks while drinking wine out of a coffee mug to look like a functional adult while chasing down her toddlers. She enjoys spending time with her family, watching reruns of Friends, and the 24/7 flow of coffee that can be found in her veins. Be sure to follow her on social media for updates on what she's working on.

You can find her here:

Facebook: https://www.facebook.com/AuthorSamanthaBaca

Instagram: https://instagram.com/author_samantha_baca

Goodreads: http://www.goodreads.com/authorsamanthabaca

Facebook Reader Group:

https://www.facebook.com/groups/2945710968775398/

Webpage: https://authorsamanthabaca.wordpress.com

Newsletter: http://eepurl.com/g0NcSj

www.ingramcontent.com/pod-product-compliance
Lightning Source LLC
Chambersburg PA
CBHW061535310726
48972CB00008B/2470